BEAUTY & THE BOARDROOM

EAGLES HOCKEY: OAK RIDGE VINEYARD #2

ELISE FABER

BEAUTY & THE BOARDROOM
BY ELISE FABER

Newsletter sign-up

BEAUTY & THE BOARDROOM
Copyright © 2025 Elise Faber
Print ISBN-13: 978-1-63749-163-8
Ebook ISBN-13: 978-1-63749-162-1

OAK RIDGE

Bottles & Blades
Beauty & the Boardroom
The Bachelor & the Break-in

ONE

Marie

I REACH for the handle of the sedan that's just pulled to a stop at the curb—

Only to find my fingers brushed away.

Starting, I jerk my head up, focus yanked from my phone, and I glare at the man who's similarly focused on his cell and, apparently, not noticing that this is my freaking car.

"What the hell are you doing?" I snap, brushing his fingers away.

He glances up, as though shocked that other people exist on Earth with him.

And given the brand of that suit—something I know because my boss, Jean-Michel Dubois, wears the same expensive designer—this man doesn't likely interact with the common people.

"What are *you* doing?" he snaps back.

"This is my Lyft."

I yank at the door, start to step into the opening.

But before I get there, his hand is on my arm, stopping me.

"Don't touch me," I growl.

He steps back, breaking contact and lifting his hands, palms out in surrender. "Fuck, woman." A scowl that does nothing to dampen the model-esque beauty of his features.

Gorgeous face.

Sexy body that fills out that expensive suit—broad shoulders, flat stomach, thick thighs.

Too bad he's an asshole.

Something he proves by what he says next.

"I don't know what mental hospital you've just checked yourself out of, but I have places to get to"—he nods at the car—"in *my* Lyft, and I don't have time to fuck around."

I glance at my phone screen then back up at the car.

The make and model match.

My app tells me my ride is here.

And this asshole is trying to take my car?

What's he even going to do when it takes him to the wrong place?

Part of me is tempted to step back and let him find out.

The rest of me is outraged.

Because I have far too much experience with men being assholes and trying to take advantage of me.

"I don't have time to 'fuck around'"—I make air quotes—"either. I have important things to do this evening too."

It's a lie.

For once, I'm not working tonight.

My plans are to soak until I'm turned into a wrinkled puddle of woman in my bathtub, drink an entire bottle of Oak Ridge wine, and then pass out with a cooking show on in the background.

But this man doesn't need to know that.

And, frankly, his destination isn't more important than mine.

I lift my phone, pointing the screen in his direction. "This is *my* ride. See?"

His expression hardens, but only for a moment before he leans in and seems to stare at my phone. He straightens, eyes flicking to the back of the car, and something strange crawls across his hazel eyes.

It almost looks like amusement.

But that can't be right because he steps back, waves a hand toward the open door, and says, "My mistake."

I scowl at him.

That's right.

It's *his* mistake.

Chin lifting, huff escaping, I dump my bag onto the seat and slide in, reaching for the door—

Only to find my fingers brushed away again.

The man pokes his gorgeous head in, one dark lock of hair falling over his face, calling for female fingers to push it back. "I'll get that for you."

Before I can reply, he's shutting it, stepping back again.

Men.

Ugh.

I sigh and start to settle back on the leather seat.

Only I freeze, horror slicing my insides to ribbons.

Because I hear the driver ask, a bit incredulously...

"Jace?"

And I realize that this isn't my car after all.

TWO

Jace

I'M JUST OPENING the other rideshare app I have on my phone to call for another car—because apparently I have a ride in progress—when a sedan pulls up to the curb, rolls down the window.

A hunch has me looking toward the driver, who asks with a confused expression, "Marie?"

Marie.

Hmm.

I wouldn't have predicted that name for the brunette with the striking green eyes.

Maybe an Amber or Felicity or Brittany.

Something akin to basic bitch.

But Marie is soft, feminine...and completely doesn't fit with the ball buster who all but kicked me out of my Lyft two minutes ago.

The car rolls forward a couple of inches and I realize I didn't answer.

"Marie is my wife," I lie, moving to the back door and reaching for the handle. I cast a surreptitious glance around, lest I steal a random Marie's car, but considering the sidewalk is empty, my instincts—and maybe the devil inside me—are telling me that I can take this leap.

I tug open the door, continue lying, "I really need to get around to making my own account, but you know how it is."

The driver chuckles and pulls away from the curb.

And…I'm committing a crime.

Well, I suppose that Marie committed a crime first.

Yup, the cops are going to love that when I'm popped for a stalking charge. I can see the headlines now—

Genen-core CEO arrested in San Francisco.

Jace Henderson, CEO and world's newest billionaire, detained on stalking charges.

Mediocre, middle-aged white dude acts like a creep.

Okay, so the last may be less headline and more reality.

Minus the mediocre part.

And middle-aged.

I'm not even thirty-five.

Did I find a gray hair the other day? Maybe. Was it my first one? No.

Do I have to consume less beer and hit it harder in the gym so my custom suits continue to fit? Yup.

Am I allowing a bunch of useless thoughts to swirl through my head?

Also…yup.

Better to think about nonsense than worry about the dismaying number of errors my executive team has made of late.

Better to think about nonsense than worry about stalking charges pressed by a feisty brunette named Marie.

Better to—

The car pulls to a stop and I blink, head swiveling, eyebrows pulling together in confusion.

At least until I spot that spicy brown-haired woman getting out of *my* Lyft.

Marching up to the front doors of *my* building.

"All good?" the driver asks and I jerk myself out of my surprise—out of the growing realization that what I thought was merely a chance meeting is going to be something far more.

I watch the sleek emerald silk of her dress flirt with her lush ass as she stalks up to the entrance.

Yeah.

Far, *far* more.

"All good," I say, unbuckling and sliding out of the back seat. "Thanks, man."

I pop the door, climb out into the warm late summer evening, and inhale deeply. We're in a busy part of the city, high rise residential buildings mingling with tech company campuses. There's an eclectic mix of restaurants and shops and chain stores, along with a wide lake encircled by a walking path. Tonight it'll be mostly empty, aside from the odd after-date couple taking a stroll. In the morning, though, it'll be full of parents pushing strollers and people walking dogs and joggers getting their run in before work.

It's a nice place to grow up.

Far nicer than anywhere I grew up, that's for damned sure.

Marie and her pretty emerald silk dress, her strappy high-heeled sandals, her shining brown curls have paused by the keypad. Her head is bent, hands searching through her purse.

"Where's the doorman?" I ask, once I've made it so close to her that I can smell the soft floral notes of her perfume.

She jumps a full foot in the air, elbow hitting me in the gut when she spins my way.

I bite back my grunt, peer beyond her into the lobby, seeing the security desk is empty too.

What the fuck?

Making a mental note, I start to reach for my wallet.

"What the fuck are you doing?" Marie snaps, glaring up at me.

I extract my wallet from my pocket, stare down into those gorgeous green eyes of hers.

Not pure green, but there are also threads of gold and brown mixing with the shades of emerald, ivy, and sea foam.

Pretty, pretty eyes...

That are sparking in anger at me.

"What do you mean?" I ask innocently.

"You're following me," she grits out. "That's creepy as hell. I'm not interested. Will *never* be interested. Now get the fuck out of here."

"Stop and think for a minute, cookie." It takes everything in me to not tug at one of those bouncy brown curls and release it, watch it spring back into shape. "You took *my* car." I lean down. "A car that brought you to this particular building."

Her eyes flare.

But I don't stop, just bend a little closer, the scent of her surrounding me, *intoxicating* me. "Want to take a stab at deducing the reason why that is?"

Her mouth drops open.

Then closes.

Then opens again.

And I decide to take advantage of the fact that I've clearly gotten her discombobulated.

I open my wallet, pull out my keycard, and swipe.

Then get to watch those pretty eyes spark with annoyance all over again when the door unlocks.

THREE

Marie

WHAT IS HAPPENING RIGHT NOW?

Like…what in the *actual* fuck is happening right now?

But I don't have time to truly process that question because he's swiping his card over the after-hours keypad—and I feel it's important to point out that it's not after-hours and our doorman should be here to let me into the fucking building.

So, you know, I don't have to be standing here, having this awkward interaction.

With the man whose rideshare I stole.

With the man who's unbelievably attractive and who I realized on the uncomfortable ride over—for I was sitting in the truth of my behavior—dropped a boatload of cash on a cake auction at the benefit I was attending for my boss this evening.

Jean-Michel can't stand the chitchat that's barely disguised as someone with their hand held out, ready to accept his black AmEx (with the intention to max it out), but that doesn't mean he hoards his money like some demented Scrooge McDuck.

He donates to a lot of causes—including the one funding a new women's health center at a local hospital that I attended tonight on his behalf and several pet charities that his daughter, Chrissy, and a woman who may as well be his daughter by now, Rory, run. He's generous with both his time and his wallet. He just...doesn't have patience for the glad-handing.

So, I do it.

I don't mind.

Dressing up is fun.

Charging a gorgeous gown to the company account (and shoes and makeup and a hairstylist's services) once or twice a quarter is a fun side perk.

Plus, it gives me a chance to scope out the competition.

Those who might try and slide in on Jean-Michel's connections, those who might try to outcompete or sabotage him.

Or those who may be a nice compliment to his corral of businesses.

Like Jace.

Who I realized on the ride over—and thanks to the power of Google—looked familiar because he's actually Jace Henderson, CEO of one of the fastest growing companies in the United States.

He's in biomed with a focus on the technological side and... it goes without saying that he is one of those business people who may be a compliment to Jean-Michel.

In fact, I'm pretty sure we have a current contract at Titan Capital with his company, Genen-core.

Which is...

Well, a fucking nightmare, isn't it?

The possibility of—after the events of this evening—having to interact with this man at my place of work.

Added on top of living in the same building as me, apparently.

Not *apparently*, I realize a moment later, catching the door before it latches shut, pulling it wide enough for me to step through...to step through and watch, Donnie, our evening security guard stroll back into the lobby and call out, "Hey, Jace!"

He extends his hand and Jace doesn't hesitate to shake it.

Ugh.

It'd be easier if he was an asshole who ignored Donnie, who barely acknowledged someone lower in social standing than him—adding to the image I created of the jerk outside the venue.

Instead, he pauses, shakes hands, and asks Donnie about his family.

He's personable, not really rubbing in the whole Lyft fiasco thing when he had every right to, and...he donates money at a charity event in an absurd auction for a cake he didn't touch benefitting women's health.

Ugh.

I want to hate him. I *need* to hate him.

"Check it out, man," Donnie says, reaching behind the counter. He snags a picture, shows it to Jace. "She just had senior prom." A shake of his head. "My little girl is all grown up."

"You give that date of hers the side eye so he'd behave?"

"More like showed him the side *arm* so he'd behave and have her back by eleven."

Jace chuckles, and I decide that it's beyond time for me to slink across the lobby and do my best to allow the floor to swallow me up as I wait for an elevator to my floor.

Unfortunately, the moment I start walking forward, I curse my gorgeous, stupidly expensive heels.

Because the *click-click* draws the attention of both men.

Jace's hazel eyes whip toward me, closely followed by Donnie's brown ones.

"Hi, Ms. Austen. You look as beautiful as my baby girl last night."

Which means that, somehow, I find myself obliged to stride forward, to lean close to the desk and take the photo he holds out.

He's not wrong.

"She's a beauty," I say softly.

"Just like her mama," he replies.

I carefully pass him back the picture. "Those college applications come back?"

He nods. "She's heading to UCSD."

"Wow," I say. "Congratulations to you both."

He grins proudly and I make my retreat, far too aware that Jace's gaze tracks my movements. Far too aware of him asking, "Where's Frank?"

Our surly doorman.

"He called off again."

Tension and disapproval in the air. "That's unacceptable."

Considering the monthly maintenance fees we pay, I can't disagree with him.

Still, that's management's issue to deal with.

I reach the elevators, jab at the button, willing it to come immediately.

Of course it doesn't.

Of course it only pings, announcing its arrival...right as the air around me shifts and changes, gathering tightly enough to make my bare skin prickle with goose bumps.

Even before I glance up, I know that he's there.

That Jace Henderson is coming close again.

"Gonna take that ride, cookie?"

Why do I think about climbing on top of him, both of us naked, and having the ride of my life?

Probably because I'm a glutton for punishment.

He crouches a little, those hazel eyes holding mine. "Gorgeous"—I resist melting when that warm word slides down my spine—"get on the elevator."

It's an order, albeit a gentle one.

But that command snaps me out of my stupor.

Christ, I'm acting like an idiot.

Lifting my chin, I step onto the car. He follows a half second later and a heartbeat after that, the doors slide closed.

Leaving me trapped with him.

Yup. This is a nightmare.

He lifts an arm, presses a button on the control panel.

"What floor?" he asks.

I blink, momentarily distracted by the way his suit caresses the ridges and valleys of his chest, his shoulders, his arms. "Wh-what?"

"I asked what floor you're on, cookie."

Fuck. I'm still acting like an idiot. Shoving that down, I grind my teeth together, lean forward, and jab at the button for my floor.

Or I start to, anyway.

Because I make it about halfway there before I realize...

The button for the top floor has already been pushed.

My head whips toward Jace's. He's got an expectant expression on his face, and confusion is creeping in.

Probably because it's not that hard to name a number or press a button.

It's just...my floor is pushed already.

By him.

Because he's going to *his* floor.

Which, apparently, is *my* fucking floor.

Nightmare. Yup.

This is a total freaking nightmare.

FOUR

Jace

THE UNIVERSE IS FUCKING with me.

Or maybe…it's on my side.

Like *really* on my side.

Because I seem to know something that Marie doesn't.

There are only two apartments on this floor—the top floor. One is mine, a penthouse suite that takes up three-quarters of the level. The other…I fight a smile as we get off the elevator, as I trail her down the hall to the door closest to us.

And she glares at me over her shoulder the whole way.

"I don't need you to walk me to my door," she grinds out.

"I know," I say, still lazily trailing her. "But it turns out that my door"—I jerk my chin beyond her—"is after yours."

She follows my stare.

Then turns back to glare at me.

"Well then"—a little dismissive wave of her hand—"feel free to get on with it."

I smirk, start to move by her. Then stop. "You know—"

She sighs, hand falling away from the electronic keypad above the door. "No," she mutters. "I *don't* know. But you're sure as shit going to tell me."

My smirk widens, and I lift a shoulder and drop it in an impassive shrug. Then I go on like she hasn't spoken the acerbic words. I don't think telling her that her glaring up at me like a pissed-off kitten is going to go over well. "You know," I say again, "I think it's kind of interesting that there are only two condos on this level. Mine and yours," I add indolently when her eyes narrow further. "And I've never so much as bumped into you before."

She scowls, turns back to the door.

When I don't immediately start walking, she says to the wooden panel, "Move along, Mr. Creepy."

I snort.

Take a step back. Stop. Can't resist asking, "Want to tell me why that is?"

"Why *what* is?"

"Why I've never run into you before, cookie."

She spins to face me, crossing her arms over her chest. "What's with that?"

"With what?"

She lifts an eyebrow. "*Cookie?*"

I just grin. "Seems we both have questions." I turn away, take a step.

"I just moved in a week ago."

"Ah," I try to keep the note of triumph out of my voice...and I have the feeling I don't succeed—or at least not completely. "That explains it."

"Explains what?"

"I was on a work trip last week."

"Oh."

A shrug. "That's why I wasn't here when you moved in."

"You keep track of everyone's comings and goings?"

I shrug again. "I like to know my neighbors." I wink, amusement curling through me when I practically see the smoke streaming out of her ears. "Or rather, *neighbor*."

Her lips part as she leans closer, and I brace myself for her retort.

This will be good.

I know it will be.

Hell, even my dick twitching in my pants knows as much.

I shift a little closer, back in range of that intoxicating perfume of hers. Cherry blossoms? Jasmine? Lavender?

"You know, *neighbor*," she begins, "I think—"

My cell rings.

Loud and clear and ruining the moment.

I wish I could say that this is the first time my phone ringing has ruined a moment for me.

Alas, that wouldn't be true.

"You'd better get that," Marie finishes, turning back to the door, punching at the keypad.

I see the code—something she should be more careful about —and file the bit of information away. Not saying I'm going to use the knowledge to my advantage...

But I'm not *not* going to use it to my advantage either.

"Night, cookie."

I don't get the chance to see her green eyes flare with annoyance because my cell rings again and at the same time, I hear the *whir* of her door's lock disengaging.

Then the slam of her door closing behind her.

Stifling a sigh, I dig out my phone, leave the confusing, perplexing, *interesting* woman to her evening and answer the call.

It's not a good one.

And I've had too many *not* good ones of late.

At first small things—issues with a production facility we're building, then a competitor swooping in and undercutting us on a bid, emails that weren't replied to and, apparently, when we reached out, had never been received.

Shit that isn't on my radar, that my team handles for me.

But eventually, so many missteps that it was brought to my attention.

Someone is trying to sabotage us.

Not entirely something that's out of the realm of possibilities in a world of corporate espionage and cutthroats.

But still annoying as fuck.

And now, I'm on the receiving end of calls at eight P.M. on a Saturday night.

Fun times being the big boss.

"Hey," I say after I swipe my finger across the screen and lift my phone to my ear. "What's happening?"

"The Duarte contract."

I frown. That's one of our biggest government contracts. "What's going on with it?"

Tom, my assistant, sighs. "Apparently, we didn't comply with the necessary environmental reports."

That's bullshit.

Something I also say aloud.

"Bullshit."

"Yes," Tom agrees as I walk around the corner, jab at the buttons on the keypad above the handle on my door. "But I think we're going to have to fly to DC to resolve this in person."

I don't want to hear that.

Not after discovering that the other apartment on my floor houses a spicy brunette with a gorgeous face and an even more gorgeous ass—

"Boss?"

I blink, realize my door is open...and that my assistant is waiting for my answer.

"I'll pack a bag," I mutter. "And meet you at the airport in an hour."

FIVE

Marie

IT'S BEEN a week since the unfortunate run-in with Jace and the Lyft.

Since *I* created the unfortunate run-in, that is.

But it's been a long week—one filled with my job as the executive vice president of Titan Capital and pretty much nothing else. Because Titan Capital is under attack.

By my boss's pernicious ex-wife.

Angela Rosseau is a piece of work, a pain in the ass, and a complete and total bitch, all wrapped up in one shiny package.

And she's been targeting Jean-Michel's, said boss's, businesses.

First, it was dropping multiple lawsuits onto his lap. Then it was showing up at his house—and his daughter, Chrissy's, house—spreading her witchliness around in the form of planting cameras and microphones for some idiotic reason. Now it's...deeper. Preying on our employees, being investigated by the FBI for having ties to an organized crime ring that is accused of kidnapping and human trafficking, and less scarily, trying to undercut our business connections.

Which means more work for Jean-Michel.

Which *means* more work for *me*.

Something I normally love.

Work is my love language—it's the part of my life that's given me the most peace and satisfaction and strength.

Jean-Michel is a tough boss, outwardly grouchy and hard to please.

But he's fair and safe and...a giant teddy bear under all that bluster.

My fairy godfather—a nickname I didn't dare to give him... but also a nickname I've found myself using, mainly because Chrissy and his unofficially adopted daughter, Rory, tease him with it on the regular.

And also because...he *is* that for me.

It's a tale as old as time.

Bad parents. Bad boyfriend.

A grumpy, taciturn boss with a heart of gold who rides in to save the day.

Now, I'm out of company housing, out of my asshole of a boyfriend's crosshairs, and I'm living on my own.

Down the hall from Jace Henderson.

Who's as talkative as Jean-Michel isn't and who seems to enjoy pushing my buttons, if our short interaction is indicative of his personality.

And my gut tells me it is.

Tells me that Jace Henderson is trouble with that sexy, muscled body, that beautiful face, that smirk I wanted to smack —or maybe kiss—off his face, all wrapped up in a gorgeous package that seems destined to tempt.

Not me.

Okay, fine. *Me*.

Certainly me, if the way he's been haunting my dreams all week is any indication.

Get naked for me, cookie.

Spread those legs for me, gorgeous.

Take it all, beautiful.

Heat flutters through my middle, dips down between my thighs, and I bite back a groan as I ride the elevator up from the parking garage. The only good thing about sharing the floor with Jace is that the CEO of Genen-core seems to travel a lot for work.

I haven't caught a glimpse of that sexy body, that annoying smirk, those gorgeous eyes...

Not since he murmured, "Night, cookie," and meandered down the hall.

Something else I've heard in my dreams.

I shiver as the elevator doors open with a ding and step out into the hall, and I'm so lost in that tempting package of rough and dangerous, silky soft and full of mischief that I don't really process what I'm seeing.

Not until the toes of my expensive—and uncomfortable—spike heels (a choice of footwear I've deemed necessary to hold my own with all the men I deal with on a daily basis) land in a puddle.

Splash!

It's the splash that does it.

Because the hallway floor is carpet.

And that's not supposed to make a splashing sound.

Slowly, and with dawning horror, I glance down.

Water.

A fuck-ton of water, at least an inch, is sitting on top of the carpet, pouring out the thin opening beneath the door, creating that puddle I splashed into.

"Oh, my God," I say, finally processing the shitshow that is happening beneath my feet.

I jab the buttons on the keypad, hearing the *whir* as the lock disengages, and then I'm yanking at the handle, shoving my way inside.

"Oh, my God!" I say again.

It's worse than I thought.

My apartment, the one I've worked hard to move into over the last few weeks—complete with careful placement of furniture and throw rugs and a shoe rack that's floating off my brand-new hardwood floor—is flooded.

Completely flooded.

I blink as my shoe rack drifts toward the front door, but I don't watch it drift out into the hallway.

Because I'm in crisis mode, trying to figure out where the leak is coming from.

The kitchen seems the most obvious culprit.

But the sink's not on and there isn't water flowing out from beneath it.

The dishwasher isn't overflowing. Hell, it isn't even hooked up—something I discovered two days ago when I tried to run a load of dishes and ended up having to wash and dry them by hand. The fridge doesn't have an ice maker, so no leak there.

I hurry down the hall to the bathroom.

The tub's not overflowing, and the shower's not on.

But the sink...

Yup, I can hear the rushing sound of water from behind the vanity doors.

Steeling myself, I pull one side open and—

"Shit!" I hiss as water flows anew, frosty cold and furious, dumping over the toes of my heels, probably ruining them, but I have bigger problems to solve.

Because I don't know how to shut it off.

There seems to be a waterfall pouring from the back of the cabinet and—

"What the hell is going on, cookie?"

I gasp, not having heard Jace come up behind me.

"I-I—" My mouth opens and closes, and all I can do is point at the vanity, at the flood of water and say blithely, "It's leaking."

His gaze was on the water pouring out, but my words have them flicking to mine for a brief moment, and I don't miss the incredulity—and blip of humor—in his hazel eyes. But I lose that connection just as quickly because he looks away, tugging off his suit jacket and hooking it on the towel holder.

Then he's—

"I—"

Too late.

He's dropping down to the tile, laying on his back as he shimmies beneath the sink, broad shoulders barely fitting into the opening.

There's a moment of stillness, the water still pouring, and then I'm watching the material of his button down strain over his torso as he does something I can't see underneath the vanity.

Something that works, though.

Because the water shuts off.

And then I'm watching a sexy—and wet, his clothes absolutely plastered to his body—Jace Henderson shimmy his way back out from beneath my sink.

And, unfortunately for me, he's wearing that smirk as he says,

"Now what, cookie?"

SIX

Jace

"I CAN'T STAY HERE!"

I'm tired.

Wet.

Pissed that I came home to an inch of water in the hallway and even more pissed that it was originating from Marie's freshly refurbished unit.

I don't want to think of the damage to the condos on the next floor down.

Don't want to think about what other hidden problems may be lurking in her place, ready to fuck up her life.

I just want to change my clothes, collapse into bed, and sleep for the next ten hours without interruption.

I know I'll be lucky to get five.

DC was a shit show. London was no better. And when I came back to California, I got to face off with several unhappy board members.

The share price.

It's always the fucking share price.

Which means that my pet project, one of the few things I've been clinging to as my business grew and the small details slipped further and further out of my day-to-day control, is on the chopping block.

When profits decline, projects that don't make a lot of money—that will likely *never* make a lot of money but are something I'm passionate about for the greater good—get cut.

That's the reality.

Before Genen-core was publicly traded, it wasn't.

I could put resources and funding toward things that were important to me.

That could be life-changing to others.

Not that our products aren't helpful.

It's just...I have a dream to do serious work on diseases that are overlooked, like endometriosis and POTS and MS.

Diseases that my mom had.

Who would have reacted exactly the same way at the order I just issued to Marie.

Which is why I'm not impatient—though I am tired and wet and ready to pass out—when I say, "Cookie, your condo is under several inches of water right now. It's late and the restoration guys are going to be working"—right on cue, an industrial vacuum turns on, echoing through the walls—"all night. Just sleep in my guest room, and we'll deal with whatever we have to deal with in the morning."

She opens her mouth, and I feel it, the sliver of impatience, of resentment at having to have this battle now, when my life is complicated and messy and I'm fucking tired.

I hate it.

Hate the feelings it invokes.

The *guilt*.

"Up to you," I say carefully, catching the strands of that

frustration and setting the bag we'd packed with some of her dry clothes on the floor by my front door. "The guest room is the first door on the left. There's a shower in there with towels, if you want to use it. Feel free to help yourself to anything in the kitchen."

I turn for the hall, and wet socks leaving footprints on the hardwood, walk to my bedroom.

Once inside the closed door, I lean back against the wood and sigh. Then I strip down, shoving my wet clothes in the hamper before I jump into the shower.

Even as I'm shampooing my hair, I hear my phone buzzing.

And it continues to go off as I rinse it out, as I soap up, as I crank off the water and dry my body.

Christ.

I wrap my towel around my waist, pick my phone up from the counter and scroll through the messages, hoping that they'll be nothing important, even as I know they are.

Dumb hope.

It's why I'm pulling on a pair of sweats and a tee, padding out on bare feet to the kitchen.

Food first.

I need sustenance to make it through what will, no doubt, be several more trying hours.

I pour a bowl of cereal, start shoveling it into my mouth, and only then do I allow myself to look toward the door.

The bag is gone.

I sigh, shake my head, pull out my laptop, and start putting out fires even as I'm silently cursing stubborn fucking women.

Screech!

I jerk my head up at the sound of hinges that need oiling—considering the guest room in my place is rarely used—and my gaze goes down the hall.

There's a sliver of light and footsteps and...

Christ, she's beautiful.

Shining brown hair curling softly around her shoulders, face scrubbed clean of makeup, cheeks pink from what I presume is her time in the hot shower—

And that's not helpful.

Because then I'm thinking about her *taking* a shower.

I'm thinking about her being *naked* in said shower and—

She falters slightly, missing a step.

Probably because I'm staring at her like she's something I want to devour.

Lush curves encased in silky black pajama pants, a gray tank peeking out from beneath a black hoodie. Simple clothes... but on that tempting body? They're sin personified.

"You stayed," I say and manage to do it sounding relatively normal.

At least it gets her moving again, feet clad in fuzzy white socks moving soundlessly on the floor.

Her nose wrinkles. "Turns out that you're right."

The acerbic tone makes me smile. "How's it feel admitting that?"

"Like chewing glass instead of bubblegum."

I laugh then push up from my stool. "You hungry?"

"No," she says, "I'm fine." Except the last word is drowned out by her stomach growling.

I laugh again. "Liar." Then, before she can protest, I open a cabinet and pull out a bowl. "I've been out of town all week so the situation in my fridge is kind of dire, but I have milk and plenty of cereal." I tug open the pantry door, gesture at the boxes on the shelf.

Silence is my only response.

And when I process that, I spin back to face her, see that her mouth has dropped open.

"Holy processed sugar, Batman," she murmurs. "Do you have a thing against real food?"

"This *is* real food."

She shifts by me, giving me a hint of that floral scent. I know it's not from the products in my spare bathroom, so it must just be...her.

Flowers and spice.

"Frosted Sugar O's?" She pulls out the box, turns it so she can read the nutritional label. "Oh! Only one-hundred-and-twenty percent of your daily recommended serving of sugar. For a half cup. Wow, what densely packed nutrition! However can your body need anything else?"

"Anyone ever tell you you're a smart ass?" I ask, snagging the box and refilling my bowl.

Sugar or not, I'm fucking hungry.

And there's nothing better than cereal at night.

"Oh, all the time," she says, bending over, searching the shelves, and pulling out...Jesus Christ, a box of the healthy cereal the girl who buys my groceries threw in a couple months back—one that I've never opened.

I shake my head.

But it's mostly so I don't swat that sweet ass of hers, just to see how she'd respond.

She pushes by me, and I hear the rattle of cereal hitting the porcelain bowl, turn to face her. She's eyeing my carton of milk like it's the spawn of Satan.

"It's not oat or almond or some shit," I mutter.

Her mouth tips up. "You said your fridge was empty, I'm checking to see if it's expired."

"It's not."

"I'll be the judge of that, thank you very much."

It's her smile that does it—prideful, mischievous, a hint of sweet.

It's her smile that unravels everything.

SEVEN

Marie

ONE SECOND, he's grinning, laughing along with my teasing.

The next, his expression flattens out, goes completely blank, hazel eyes turning cold and hard, amusement gone.

My mind screeches to a halt.

What the hell happened?

What the hell did I say?

"Are you—?"

He blinks and charming is back...albeit behind a thick wall of ice. "Enjoy the cereal," he murmurs, reaching for his bowl, his laptop and phone. "I need to do some work so I'll just catch up with you later. Let me know if you need anything."

"Jace—"

He's already striding away, barely pauses to glance back at me over his shoulder. "Yeah?"

A terse question.

And I'm reminded that I don't know this man at all.

The circles beneath his eyes are a dark black, the lines around his face and mouth heavy and deep.

Some weird urge has me wanting to tell him to not stay up too late.

An even weirder one has me wanting to close the distance between us and hug him tightly.

I don't do either of those things.

Instead, I find myself saying, "Thanks for the cereal."

A flicker of humor, of light in those hazel eyes, and for a moment, I think I'm going to break through.

But he just replies with, "You're welcome," before disappearing down the hall.

And as I sit in the empty kitchen, slowly polishing off my bowl of cereal, all I can think is that I really should have gone with the Frosted Sugar O's.

Because this healthy stuff tastes like shit.

Hours LATER, I prop open Jace's door and move down the hall.

The vacuums haven't run for at least a half hour and the lights are dim, the space quiet except for an odd humming sound.

So, I take the chance to look, to see if maybe I *can* sleep in my own bed after all.

But what I find isn't exactly conducive to that.

The cleaners are gone and while they've mopped up most of the water, they've also opened all the windows and brought in a bunch of big ass fans that are currently creating a wind tunnel in my condo.

It's damp and loud and freezing cold.

No, I won't be sleeping here tonight.

The question is, though, should I sleep in Jace's guest room?

I could call Jean-Michel or Chrissy or Rory. They would offer up hospitality in a second. But...they're newly coupled up, just starting their happily ever afters, they don't need me cramping their style.

And anyway, I don't need to be across town in the morning.

I need to be here, down the hall, ready to deal with this mess bright and early.

So, I close and lock the door, pad back to Jace's condo, doing the same there, though I pause before I head to the guest room and peel off my now wet socks. But when I start forward again, I realize the hems of my pajama pants are wet too, leaving trails of moisture on his gorgeous hardwood floor.

I pause just inside the guest bedroom and push them down, leaving me in my oversized hoodie, underwear, and tank.

Then turn for the bathroom, intending to hang them and my socks up to dry.

It's my turn that has me spotting it.

Hearing it.

The faint sound of music. The narrow bead of light.

Curiosity...

Well, I guess it got the cat *and* me.

I move toward the music, toward the light, and—

My breath hitches when I catch sight of him, his big body sprawled out on a brown leather couch...sleeping.

And he looks...

Peaceful and beautiful and I don't know why, but my feet carry me forward, carry me toward that big couch and the sleeping man on top of it.

I stop when my toes bump against the leather, and it's only then that I realize how close I've come, how creepy I'm acting (oh, the irony). I slam the lid on my curiosity—and on my *creepy* —and start to retreat.

Only...he looks so much younger like this, eyes closed, lashes casting shadows on the tops of his cheeks, face relaxed, those lines around his mouth, scattered on his temples softer. Quiet and peaceful and a little disheveled, his clothes wrinkled, locks of hair having fallen forward, draping over his forehead.

I should turn away.

Should leave and go to the guest room.

Hell, I should leave Jace's condo all together and get a fucking hotel room.

But, for some reason, I can't make myself.

For some reason, I can't stop myself from reaching forward and smoothing back those hairs.

They're soft, way softer than I expect and maybe that's why I don't immediately lift my hand, why instead of doing what's prudent, I start sliding my fingers through his hair, sifting through the locks. I memorize the texture, the feel of them shifting over my hand, the even cadence of his breath and slow and steady rise and fall of his chest.

I linger, soaking it all in.

It's dangerous.

Dumb.

Yet, I can't stop.

I just keep stroking, just keep my feet planted, my mind focused on this small thing.

Keep touching Jace Henderson.

Until my phone buzzes in the pocket of my hoodie and...

I process how truly insane I'm acting right now.

Only then do I jerk my hand away, a gasp bubbling up in my throat. I barely manage to stifle it as I skitter back a step, as I turn to leave—

His arm snakes out, hand clasping the top of my bare thigh, and this time, my gasp *does* escape.

Cheeks flaring hot, embarrassment seeping out of each and every one of my pores, I glance down, see that his eyes are open, and an apology forms on my lips. "I-I'm—" But that's as far as I get.

Just as well, anyway.

Because he takes over on the speaking front.

His voice is rumbly, a little drowsy when he asks,

"Why'd you stop?"

EIGHT

Jace

I EXPECT to face fire and barbed wire.

Yeah, she was the one who was touching me first.

Still, I expect a verbal retort.

Maybe even a physical one—a hand covering mine, bending back my finger until I have to release that succulent thigh or risk a broken bone. Maybe a kick to the balls, nails clawing at my face.

What she gives me...

Is anything but that.

Her hand covers mine, stroking light fingertips over the back, lifting goose bumps on my flesh, making my cock go hard.

Hell, who am I kidding?

It already was hard, waking from a dream of this woman to find her standing over me, touching me, half naked and close and smelling like flowers.

And running her fingers through my hair.

Fuck, but I love it when a woman strokes her fingers through my hair.

Of course, I'd love it even more if she'd stroke something else.

I open my mouth to suggest that, but don't get the chance to as her hand keeps moving, trailing along the inside of my arm, over my shoulder, across my chest.

"You work out."

Not a question.

But I still want to answer it, anyway, still want to preen like a fucking peacock and tell her exactly how much I can bench press, squat, and deadlift, all at once.

I don't, though.

Mostly because her hand shifts, sliding up, cupping the side of my neck.

"And your hair is soft."

More preening.

More wanting to turn into that puffed-up peacock.

"Come here, cookie," I murmur instead, tugging lightly at her thigh, stroking my fingers up a little higher.

Tempting heat.

Silky skin.

I get more of it when she heeds my tug and clambers on top of me.

"What happened to your pants?" I ask gruffly.

Her eyes come to mine—molten emerald—and then drift away, cheeks heating, knees buckling. She settles on top of me with a quiet gasp, and the weight of her is welcome. So is the heat of her pussy burning through her underwear. "They got wet."

I slide a hand up, dip my fingers between her legs. "How?"

She squirms slightly, pressing against me, telling me enough. She's as turned on as I am.

"The same way these are wet, gorgeous?" I ask, continuing to stroke.

That emerald gaze flies back to mine and I half expect her to shy away.

But who am I kidding?

I haven't been good at predicting what the hell this woman is going to do, not from the moment she stole my Lyft out from right under my nose.

So, instead of getting shy, instead of hiding and curling up in embarrassment because I caught her creeping on me while I was sleeping, she's on top of me, her hands on either side of my face, mouth curving into a grin that's filled with naughtiness.

"How do you think they got wet, handsome?"

"Because you were thinking about me?"

Laughter, bright and musical rings out. "What makes you say that?"

I sit up in a rush, flipping us on the couch, glad as fuck that I bought the one that was big enough so we don't topple to the floor.

Instead, I get to enjoy this.

Curves beneath me. Long legs wrapped around my hips.

A beautiful woman staring up at me in befuddlement.

"Told you I work out," I say blithely.

That befuddlement disappears like a puff of smoke and then I get that beautiful laughter again. "I think I was the one who made that statement."

"Well," I say, hips flexing ever so carefully, groan rising in the back of my throat when it presses against the softness between her legs. I bite it back, just barely. "You're not wrong."

Her mouth kicks up. "Are we really going to keep talking when you're hard and on top of me?"

"I thought women liked to talk."

"And *that's* why you're single."

I'm the one who laughs this time, loud and unbothered, then again when her nose wrinkles.

"What?" I ask, smoothing a fingertip along those ridges.

"You're supposed to be offended."

I shrug. "Not much offends me."

"Hmm." She tilts her head to the side, studying me like I'm a bug. "Stolen Lyfts don't seem to bother you."

"Convenient that the one *I* stole brought me where I needed to go."

"And neither do flooded condos."

"Wasn't my condo that got flooded."

"But for some reason, me teasing you about sugary cereal does?"

Guilt for the way I acted earlier coils through my middle—worse because she thinks it had something to do with her and not the fucked-up childhood demons that sit heavy on my heart...so heavily sometimes that I've found it easier to be single.

Of course, I've never met a woman like Marie before.

Never been quite so obsessed.

Instead of thinking about that—or the fear that bubbles up with those words sliding through my mind—I curve my mouth into a smirk. "A man who works out doesn't like his diet to be picked apart by a woman who's all of a hundred pounds."

Eyes going wide...then narrowing. "Not that it's any of your business, but I'm a hundred and fifty pounds *and* can bench press one-ten."

"A regular Schwarzenegger," I say dryly.

Which earns me a swat on the chest.

But at least she's smiling.

"Seriously, I'm impressed."

"You should be," she mutters, but I don't miss the confusion in her eyes, as though not a lot of men in her life have given her an outright compliment.

I hate that for her.

But it's not why I answer honestly, saying, "I'm serious, gorgeous. I'm impressed."

That's just who I am. I don't play games. I go after what I want, but I don't fuck over everyone on the way up.

They say there are no ethical billionaires.

But I'm doing my damndest to have that not apply to me.

Marie's nose wrinkles adorably again and I stop thinking about society and the past and how much this impressive woman can bench press. Instead, I give in to the urge to bend down and press my lips there.

"You have freckles here."

One shoulder lifts in an approximation of a shrug. "I wasn't great about wearing sunscreen when I was younger."

"Hmm." I touch the smattering. "I like them."

"Are we still talking?"

"Considering this is the most cooperative you've been from the moment I've met you, yeah, I'd kind of like to talk to you some more, cookie."

"You could tell me why you keep calling me cookie."

"*You* could tell me why you were in my office, standing over me, stroking my hair, and generally acting like the creeper you accused me of being last week."

"Technically, it was *more* than a week ago."

"You keeping tabs on me, gorgeous?"

"Are *you* going to stop talking and get around to fucking me, handsome?"

NINE

Marie

I'VE LOST MY MIND.

I know that.

But I don't care.

He's strong and beautiful, and his body feels fucking great pressing into mine.

And his hair is silky soft and his smile is intoxicating and... it's been so *damned* long since I've allowed myself to have a moment like this.

Luckily, my words have their desired effect.

One big palm settles heavily on my hip, slides up my side, dragging the fabric of my hood and tank top with it.

But when the material bunches up just beneath my breasts, he stops, brows flicking up. "No pants *and* no bra?"

I shrug as well as I'm able, considering I'm laying down and he's pinning me in place. "The bra seemed unnecessary considering the hoodie."

"And the pants?"

"Like I said, I checked out my apartment, they got wet, and..."

"You slipped in here to creep on me."

He's not wrong.

I'll also never admit that, not even under pain of death.

"I thought we were going to fuck."

His lips twitch. "Maybe I need a little romance, cookie."

Dammit.

Why does he have to be funny?

And nice. And have the ability to save the day by turning off the water and getting management to immediately bring in the abatement crew.

I can't think about that.

Any of it.

So, I reach for my hoodie, my tank, and I yank them up and over my head.

Leaving me in just my underwear.

His big body jerks, and heat blooms in my belly. Because his eyes...holy hell, they're blazing as they drag along my front, up, up, *up* to meet mine. Where they *burn* with need. For me. "Gorgeous," he murmurs, that hand settling on my side again.

I jump, arching into his touch, lips parting on a sigh when his slightly roughened fingertips trace lightly up my torso, pausing just beneath my breasts.

They ache for him, my nipples hardened buds that call for his fingers and mouth, his lips and tongue and teeth.

But he doesn't give that to me.

Not yet.

Instead, it's just lazy patterns, light touches, delicate strokes.

"In a hurry, cookie?" he teases when my hips buck, seeking purchase.

"Yes," I snap. "For an orgasm. Think you can manage that?"

His hand flattens just beneath one breast, his mouth hitches up at one corner. "And to think," he drawls, "she hasn't even kissed me yet."

"If you weren't so handsome, I'd slap that smug look off your face."

He just grins, that smug smile growing. "If you did, then you wouldn't get *this*." He settles his pelvis against mine and I gasp as the hard edge of his erection presses against me, hips bucking, neck arching, lips parting—

Something he takes advantage of.

He drops his mouth to mine.

Now I'm not gasping. I'm moaning.

Because the man can *kiss*.

He gives no quarter, no mercy, just settles his mouth on mine and kisses me like I'm his last breath. His tongue delves deep, tangling with mine, lips working. His hand dives into my hair holding me in place while he plunders, his hips grinding against mine, his big body pressing me into the couch.

That's good but—

I hook a leg around his waist and we both groan.

Because, yeah, that's better.

"Christ, gorgeous," he mutters against my mouth. "You really *are* in a hurry, aren't you?"

"I need a non-self-induced orgasm." I hook my other leg around his hip, groan again as that becomes even better. "Like six months ago."

He pauses in his movements, head rearing back. "Six months?"

"I've been busy," I lie, grinding against him, already feeling those curls of pleasure crawling up and surrounding me.

"Hmm," he murmurs.

My impatience begins to boil over. "Jace?"

"Hmm?"

"Am I going to need to find someone else?"

The question is barely out of my mouth before he stands up, and for one horrible second, I think he's going to tell me to get on with that finding someone else.

But then he walks over to the desk and I hear a soft *screech* as he opens a drawer.

Frowning, I push up to sitting.

Then I see it.

And I grin.

"Well?" he asks.

"What?" I reply, eyebrows dragging together.

"You going to put it to good use?"

"The condom you just pulled out or the erection tenting your pants?"

He tugs off his shirt, tosses it to the side. "Both, cookie." Then he shoves down his pants.

Heat rips through me because...

Sweet Christ.

His dick is magnificent.

Big and thick, the tip glistening with precum.

I want to drop to my knees and suck it deep. I want to wrap my hands around him and stroke until he comes apart for me. I want—

He tears open the condom wrapper, rolls it down the hard length of his cock.

Then sits down in his desk chair.

"Come here, gorgeous," he orders softly.

I melt, seriously melt, and it takes everything in me to push up to my feet, to not allow my knees to collapse as I walk over to him.

He's magnificent, that muscular chest, his flat abs, his strong thighs...his big dick.

"Underwear off," he rumbles when I come close, when I start to lift one leg.

Right.

I need to be naked too for this to work.

A push has them sailing to the floor.

He sucks in a breath and my gaze flies to his. "Fucking beautiful," he murmurs. "Every part of you."

I step close, run my hand along his chest.

"Climb on," he orders.

Yeah, I want to do that.

I clamber up onto his lap, legs straddling his, the head of his cock brushing against my pussy, sliding through the slick folds of my labia, notching at my entrance.

"Christ," he mutters. "I haven't even gotten to taste those tits yet."

Desire ripples through me, soaking the head of his cock, and I slide down an inch without really meaning too.

Then, because that feels so good, I allow myself to drop another inch.

He curses.

I grin, take another inch. Then another and another.

Until I've taken all of him and our pelvises are pressed together and we're both breathing heavily, sweat breaking out on our bodies.

"Fuck but you've got a great pussy, gorgeous."

Surprise has laughter vibrating through me and we both groan.

Because that feels good.

No, because it feels fucking *great*.

Jace settles a hand on my cheek, his eyes burning into mine when he asks,

"Ready to get to work, cookie?"

TEN

Jace

I WATCH HER FACE CHANGE.

Mischief and heat becoming more. Becoming need and urgency. The emotions in her expression burn with such intensity that I swear I get caught in the crosshairs of their flames.

And I don't give a fuck.

Because she's lifting up.

And sliding down.

And lifting up.

And sliding down.

And—

"Fuck!" I groan.

She does something with her hips that—*holy shit*—has red hazing at the edges of my vision, has sweat breaking out on my spine. Something that has my pleasure ratcheting dangerously high. A flex of graceful movement, a tightening of that sweet cunt, a swivel of her pelvis.

"Like that?" she asks breathlessly.

I clamp my hands onto her waist, thrusting up as she strokes down. "Almost as much as you do, cookie."

Her eyes flare, her rhythm falters, her pussy flutters around me.

Close.

But not close enough.

And I don't have time to continue fucking around, don't have time to learn all the little things that make her moan, that slowly undo her.

I'm too close to the edge.

So, I ask, "What do you need?"

Green eyes filled with questions.

I hold her tighter, keep driving up into her relentlessly. "What do you need to come apart?"

Molten emeralds. A convulsing pussy.

Then she takes my hand and draws it in across her stomach, down between her legs, pressing my fingers to her clit. "Here," she murmurs, rubbing it in a tight circle. "Right here. And don't stop."

I circle that hard bud of nerves, rubbing like she showed me.

Not stopping like she told me.

"Oh, God," she whispers, her head falling back. "Oh, my God. *Yes.*"

"Come for me gorgeous," I order, taking advantage of her swaying toward me to capture one hard nipple in my mouth and suck deep.

She gasps, rhythm faltering.

But only for a moment.

Because then she's grinding faster, grinding harder.

Fingers and flesh. Tongues and bouncing tits. A tight pussy. Rounded hips. Slender waist. A flash of blazing green eyes before her head drops back, a moan filling the air, her pelvis bucking, taking me deeper, so deep that I bump against her womb. But she doesn't freeze in pain, doesn't stop fucking me.

So I don't either.

I work her clit.

I suck at her nipples.

I thrust up into her.

And—

She cries out, clamping around me, and I'm able to get a glimpse of her orgasm sliding across her face before mine is on top of me.

It explodes inside of me, stronger than anything I've ever felt before.

My vision goes black on the edges, and every nerve in my body is on fire for one long moment.

Then everything melts. My limbs go lax. My brain goes hazy and I'm only distantly aware of us continuing to move together as we seek out the dredges of our orgasms.

It may be minutes or hours later before I'm able to open my eyes.

But it's longer still before I'm able to lift an arm, to lightly stroke my hand down her back. "Christ, cookie," I mutter, gathering my strength to get us out of this chair, knowing that I'm never going to look at it the same way again.

"What?" she says lazily.

"You're a fucking wildcat, aren't you?"

She chuckles and it's just as lazy. "Truthfully, I'm not feeling much of anything right now."

"I know the feeling," I say dryly.

She sighs. "That was good, wasn't it?"

"Mm-hmm." I tangle my fingers in her hair. "*Really* good."

Like the best fucking ever.

Another aggrieved sigh, her body slumping against mine.

"Want to tell me my you're acting like that's the worst thing in the world?" I ask, grunting as I haul us both out of the chair and start moving toward my bedroom. After an orgasm like that, I need to get horizontal and stay there for a good ten hours.

"Because we live down the hall from each other."

"And?"

"And"—she waves a lazy hand as I settle her on the mattress and step back—"you're not the kind of man who does connections."

My brow furrows.

Because that's true. *Normally.*

It's just with this woman that connection doesn't automatically seem like a dirty four-letter word.

"And now I have to live down the hall," she says, "knowing that you're packing what you're packing—and worse, that you know how to fucking use it—all while knowing that it can never be more than a one-time thing."

My dick's still wet from being inside her and she's talking about a one-time thing?

Jesus Christ.

She's worse than I am.

"Who's saying it can only be once?"

She sniffs, stretching out on the mattress and tugging the blanket over her. "A man like you? A man like you who looks like that, who's packing"—a wave of her hand toward my cock— "*that?* Yeah, it can only ever be a once. I'm not the kind of girl who gets off on a broken heart."

I shake my head, moving to the bathroom so I can take care of the condom. "No," I call, "you're the one who gets off on *giving* them."

Her laughter is answer enough.

I wash my hands, stride over to the bed, and yank the blankets back, ignoring her gasp as I climb over the top of her.

"What are you do—?"

I reach for the nightstand drawer, pull out a string of condoms.

"Well, if I only have one night—"

"I said one *time*—"

"—I'm going to make it count."

She starts sputtering.

But I just bend my head and kiss her...then take my time making sure the next *three* times count.

And when my lids feel heavy and sleep is barreling toward me, I tug her limp body into my arms and let it come, hoping that she's all bluster.

But in the morning I find out she's not.

Because in the morning—

I wake up and she's gone.

ELEVEN

Marie

I EXHALE and roll my shoulders, exhaustion clinging to every single cell.

I didn't get much sleep last night.

So totally worth it to have experienced all the fucking that Jace Henderson can dish out.

But I'd meant what I said last night.

It was a moment of insanity, a blip in time, an enjoyable—*very*—distraction.

That was it.

And I'm fine with that.

Even though my body is humming this afternoon, wanting another interlude, wanting more time with Jace and his very delicious self, I'm deliberately focusing on work.

Because work is safe.

Because work is the best.

Because work isn't going to turn on me the moment I fall for him...er, *it*.

The only problem is that my mind is drifting, not wanting to focus on the contract in front of me, nor the meeting prep for my check-in with Jean-Michel in a half hour.

Nor my inbox or my voicemails or clearing the insane amount of papers and files, sticky notes and pens off my desk.

My organization style is...

Chaos.

I know where everything is—just ask me and I can tell you exactly where I stowed the Post-It with important dates for distribution of product from Jean-Michel's winery, Oak Ridge Vineyards, from my meeting last week. I can locate the exact pad I took notes for a business trip to Germany next month. Same as the file for one of our new collaborators and the lunch order for our on-site on Friday.

Chaos, but organized chaos all the same.

"You look like you're a million miles away."

My gaze jerks up from my messy desk to my boss, who's standing, arms crossed, leaning back against the doorframe.

He's swapped his usual suit for a tee and jeans, telling me without actually telling me that he's spent the morning at the vineyard. I push up from my desk. "I'll run down to your office, grab your spare suit."

He waves me off, steps toward me, blue eyes searching.

And *piercing*. The man never misses a thing.

Case in point?

"You didn't get enough sleep last night."

Not a question.

A statement spoken confidently as he settles in the chair in front of my desk.

"Your meeting—"

"I'll get the suit in a minute, Marie." It's no-nonsense, and not exactly impatient, but also, he's not going to give me an inch. "Why didn't you get enough sleep last night?"

Because I fucked a man into oblivion and enjoyed every second of it.

Obviously not a fun fact I can share with my boss...who's also become a bit of a father figure.

So, I give him the other half of the truth.

"My condo flooded."

His chin jerks back, telling me that he'd expected the explanation to be similar to what we've been struggling with over the last few months—his ex-wife and her machinations against Jean-Michel's life and businesses.

"Your condo *flooded?*"

I wince. "Yup, I went home last night and the carpet was soaked in the hallway outside my front door." I explain about the several inches of water and the broken pipe beneath the sink in my bathroom, the abatement team and how I'll be staying in a hotel for a bit.

Starting tonight, that is.

Then I spend the next five minutes reassuring him that I've got this and I don't need to stay at his or Chrissy's or Rory's places.

"It's fine," I say, holding his gaze, forcing him to accept that it *is* fine—or at least that I'm not going to budge on this front. Jean-Michel is a formidable businessman but I began as merely his assistant and have worked my way up to someone who is integral to his company's day-to-day operations. And along the way, I've gained his respect and trust (and vice versa). So I know that he'll respect the line I'm drawing when I add, "I'll let you know if anything changes, but right now I have it covered, okay?"

He scowls, and I know that even though he says, "Okay," he'll be keeping an extra close eye on me.

Great.

One billionaire living next door, making no secret of the

fact that he wants an extension of our three-peat last night that left me limp and sated and aching for more. And another watching extra closely to make sure I make it back into my condo as soon as possible.

Back into temptation.

Maybe I should just move right now.

The condo is cursed.

Whose place floods within the first month of moving in?

It makes sense to pull the plug, to move on—or rather *in*—to a different place.

Only...it took me close to a year to find a property in my budget that had the amenities and location that I wanted. Starting over now...

God, I really can't even begin to fathom it.

Jace travels for work as much as I do.

The chances of our paths actually crossing on the regular has to be slim to none.

An annoying little voice in my brain says that I'm trading in delusions, but I know I can't let it win—not today, not right now, not when everything from last night is so fresh in my head, so...tempting.

I *have* to cling to the lies I'm telling myself.

Not *lies*. Truths.

Just truths that may or may not affect said delusions I'm clinging too.

Sighing, I grab my notebook I have set especially for meetings like this with Jean-Michel and snag my pen.

"All right," I say. "Quit stalling and give me the rundown on the acquisition of Rosque Enterprises."

TWELVE

Jace

I DON'T REALIZE I'm holding my breath, hoping to spot a certain brunette until I get off the elevator and slow by the open door to her condo.

But the only people inside are the construction crew.

Who've followed the abatement team.

Maybe I shouldn't have pulled strings and made sure the repair work on Marie's place started immediately.

Maybe I should have tied her to my bed and never let her up.

Maybe I should—

A saw turns on, jarring me out of my thoughts, and I start walking again, moving down the hall and jabbing at the keypad on my door.

The lock whirs, and I step inside, dropping my shit on the kitchen counter, trying to pretend my place hasn't felt empty from the moment I woke up and Marie was gone a week ago.

Trying to pretend I haven't been looking behind every

corner, every door, into every elevator car, even the chairs in the lobby, hoping to see her, to have a chance to talk to her, a chance to talk her back *up* into my apartment.

But I haven't so much as glimpsed a curl on her head.

Though, I know she's been by the building, walked through her condo with the construction team, okayed tearing out the floor and selected the replacement vanity and tile for the bathroom.

How do I know this?

Because I own the fucking building.

Which is why I know that the quickest way to get Marie's place fixed up is to pay through the nose to use my construction team so work can begin immediately.

And also maybe because using my construction team means that Mark, the general contractor, would be guaranteed to do me a solid and shoot me a text telling me that a certain spitfire was in her condo, checking on the progress to date.

I'm not embarrassed to say that I cut my meeting short and hauled ass from my office here.

Only to find an empty fucking condo.

No. *Two* empty fucking condos.

I scowl and go to the fridge, yank open the door then pull out a beer.

But even as I suck it down, as I strip off my suit and change into sweats and a tee, I'm restless.

I have work, an ever-overflowing inbox to sift through, phone calls to review, tomorrow's meetings to prep for.

But I can't bring myself to open my laptop.

To unlock my phone.

"Fuck it," I mutter, tossing it on the counter, leaving my laptop closed while I drain my beer. Then I turn back to the fridge, grab a bottle of water, and head back out into the hall. The guys are still working in Marie's place—something they'll be doing until the nightly noise ordinances kick in (something I know because I'm footing the bill for the fucking overtime). I still glance inside, still hope to catch a glimpse of her, and when I don't, I stifle a curse, move to the elevator, and jab at the button.

Once inside, I hit the floor for the gym.

Can't work, can't sleep? May as well work off that fucking beer...and maybe exhaust myself so that I don't dream of Marie's soft body and breathless moans and the tight clasp of her slick pussy. So I don't wake up with an erection that could jackhammer fucking concrete.

I sigh as the doors open, turn for the door to the gym, snagging a towel from the rack and—

Freezing.

What the fuck?

All week, all *fucking* week I've been looking for her...

And here she is, casually walking on the treadmill, her fabulous ass in tight leggings, her pert tits straining at a bra top I want to yank down so I can feast on her naked flesh.

The erection I've been fighting all day springs back to rigid attention.

Beautiful.

Intoxicating.

And staring at her phone.

Mischief flickers to life in my belly as I toss the towel over my shoulder and stroll toward the bank of treadmills, not moving quietly, and especially not doing it once I realize she's so engrossed in whatever she's reading that I could ring a fucking gong and she wouldn't look up.

I step onto the machine adjacent to hers, turn it on, and match my speed to hers.

And wait for her to notice I'm here.

And *wait.*

So, not only would she not notice a gong going off, but she might miss the next big earthquake. Maybe even a nuclear bomb.

Mischief grows into curiosity, and I lean over slightly, matching her strides, trying to see what's on the screen of her e-reader.

But the letters are too small, especially with the screen in dark mode and me bouncing along beside her.

I scowl, lean a little closer.

And almost eat shit for my trouble.

But just before I topple off the treadmill like I'm a klutzy gym-goer in a bad TikTok video (or maybe a really good one) I spot a word on the screen.

No.

I spot the word *cock* on the screen.

And I realize she's not supremely focused on a work email or a reviewing a contract.

She's reading a smutty—I lean closer, somehow managing not to catapult myself off the end of my treadmill—and I mean *smutty* book.

A grin spreads on my face.

"*This* is what you're reading?"

She jumps, eyes coming to mine, mouth dropping open...

And then she stumbles.

THIRTEEN

Marie

I GASP, losing hold of my e-reader.

It clatters to the floor...and then I realize with horror that I'm next.

That I'm going to be tumbling to the floor next.

Or face planting.

But that thought is in and out of my head in a heartbeat.

Because even as I start to fall—

I hear a beep, my motion abruptly cuts off—

And then I'm in Jace's arms.

How the fuck am I in Jace's arms?

And why does it feel so right? Why, instead of fighting his hold, am I melting against his chest, my pulse skittering for a completely different reason aside from fear?

"Sorry," he says huskily, setting me on my feet, hands holding on to my waist until I'm steady.

Then he turns, reaching up and hitting the stop button on both machines.

The belts slow, stop—same as my pulse.

But that settling doesn't come quickly enough for my sanity because by the time I'm dropping back into myself, by the time my heart stops beating against my rib cage, my brain starts working again, he's bent...

And scooped up my e-reader.

With my supremely dirty book open right there on the screen.

"I—"

To my complete and utter horror, he begins reading,

"'I want to be the one sitting on his lap, want to be the one who so confidently sinks my fingers into those dark blond locks and shoves his gorgeous face into my not-as-nice-as-hers-but-still-fucking-great breasts. Hot breath on my skin. A calloused hand skating along my side. A thick cock pushing home—'" He looks up, grins. "Jesus, gorgeous." Then keeps reading and clicking and I'm too horrified and shocked to stop him.

"'Don't be scared, little spitfire, not now that we've finally had some fun.'" Hot eyes tossed in my direction. "I know exactly what kind of fun they're talking about, cookie." His voice rumbles as he continues reading the scene—and it's a good one—out loud, "'I should threaten to stab you with my keys again.' He winds an arm around my middle. 'I might like it if it means you'll let me feel that tight pussy of yours again.'" His eyes sparkle with mirth...and heat. "Is this where you get your inspiration from?"

What kind of inspiration?

For horizontal fun—or vertical, if it involves a big desk chair and an even bigger dick? Or for my next level snark skills?

Because the correct answer to this is...yes. To both.

To so many things.

Including the many, *many* spicy dreams I've had about

repeating our nighttime adventures—and doing them in the morning, afternoon, or crepuscular hours.

The man has a magic dick.

I knew it, knew it from that first sexy smile he tossed my way.

And I'm no less immune to his charms than I've ever been.

The only difference is that I'm finally smart enough to not stick my hand into the flames and get burned by another man.

I set the boundaries.

I make the decisions.

I decide when enough is enough...so I'm not ever that vulnerable again.

"Hand it over, Henderson," I order, extending my hand, palm up.

His eyes dance with humor, but he doesn't pass me my e-reader back. Instead, he swipes...and—kill me now—keeps reading, "*'My mouth falls open and before I can find a retort—and I have to face it, one would be a long time coming.'*" He glances up, the amusement in those gorgeous eyes growing. "Wouldn't that be nice? If a certain someone's retorts were stymied..."

I grind my teeth together. "You—"

Before I can retort—and no, I don't know if one would spring free, or if I would be like the heroine in this hockey romance, struggling to keep up with the pesky hero—he goes on, "*'Especially with that smirk he's sporting and those twinkling eyes and the way his pants are just barely staying up...One tug and—'*" Wide eyes. An even wider grin as he flicks his gaze down toward his sweats...which, indeed, are barely staying up. "Wanna try that tug out in real life?"

I snort. "In your dreams."

He drops my e-reader into my hand, gently bends my fingers around the can-survive-an-atom-bomb case, and says,

"Yeah, gorgeous, in my dreams. One hundred percent, in my dreams every night since I woke up and found my bed empty."

My heart thuds hard, slamming against my ribs, stealing my breath. "I told you it was one night only."

Half of his mouth hitches up. "Yeah, cookie, you did." One big shoulder lifts, drops. "Or at least, you said it was one *time* only." The other half of his mouth curves up wickedly. "I changed your mind about that too."

"I don't want—"

"*You* don't want it," he murmurs, stepping closer. "But that doesn't mean that *I* only wanted one night."

Danger. *Danger.*

He brushes the backs of his knuckles over my cheek and the gentle touch undoes me...and simultaneously locks me into place. "I-it doesn't matter," I say, clinging to the words that thankfully slide off my tongue without me really thinking about them, growing stronger with each one I speak. "I wanted it to be one night, so it's one night."

I expect a reply.

Expect him to push back.

Instead, he stands there, steady and still and silent for three —I count—heartbeats. Then he drops his hand to his side and steps back.

I hate that he's no longer touching me, hate more that he's stepped back.

But a mere *five*—again, I count—heartbeats after he retreats that pace away, I'm contemplating murder.

Because he whips off his shirt, tosses it on the handle of the treadmill, and glances over his shoulder at me, eyes sparking with a challenge I feel the inner teenager in me unable to back down from.

"Okay, then," he says easily as he begins pushing at the control panel on the treadmill.

I frown, trying my best to not drool over that gloriously naked torso, glistening lightly with sweat in the overhead lights. Narrow hips I wrapped my legs around as he pounded into me, a muscular back I dug my nails into, an ass I wanted to bite.

"Okay what?" I push out when I realize he's still watching me, presumably waiting for a reply.

His eyes dance.

His grin reappears.

His question has me plotting homicide by dumbbell.

Because then he asks,

"So, how far are we running, cookie?"

FOURTEEN

Jace

THE DOOR SLAMS against the wall, probably denting it, maybe leaving a hole in the sheetrock.

But I don't give a fuck.

Because Marie's legs are wrapped around my waist and her mouth is locked onto mine, her tongue delving deep. Because I've got my hands on that lush ass as I kick the door closed and pin her back against it.

"This is stupid," she puffs out as I drag my lips along her jaw, down her throat, taking advantage of all the bared skin on her chest and arms and middle to trace my tongue and lips along the silky flesh, the tempting curves.

"This is the best idea you've ever had," I say against her skin, nipping lightly, flicking out my tongue.

Tasting her.

Devouring her.

"Stupid," she repeats, her fingers tightening in my hair, her body arching against mine. "But it's still really fucking great."

I don't argue with that, just reach down and wrap my fingers around the hem of her shirt, start yanking it up. It catches on her breasts, but I just yank harder, my tugs rewarded when her tits pop out. "Christ, you're fucking beautiful," I growl, burying my face in those gorgeous tits, licking and sucking, squeezing and rolling the hard buds of her nipples on my tongue. Loving the sounds of her moans, the feel of her rocking against me, shuddering when her hands snake down between us, dive into the waistband of my sweats and she wraps her fingers around my cock.

I curse.

She grins and starts stroking, and I know that I'm not all that far from losing control—or coming in my pants like a teenager, so I do some snaking and shoving of my own, knocking her hands away, using my body to pin her against the wall so I can get my hand in those leggings.

Peeling them down her legs is like wrestling a fucking crocodile, but I eventually manage to pull them, her underwear, and her shoes off.

I leave the socks.

Because they're cute.

Which sends a blip of alarm through me.

Cute isn't hot. Cute isn't sexy. Cute is more...leading to obsession, to connection, to—

Her nails bite into my scalp, slicing through the sudden burst of panic.

Right.

Who am I kidding?

I've been bordering on obsession from the moment she blocked me from getting in the Lyft.

Pretending otherwise is insanity.

But going down this road—

Is just as crazy.

Because what if—

"You going to stare at my pussy all day?" she murmurs, her tone breathless, albeit teasing. "Or are you going to make me feel good, handsome?"

I rip myself out of my thoughts, slam the heavy, steel door on the past.

Not the fucking time.

"You've got a gorgeous cunt, cookie." I slide a finger through the plump, slick folds. "I kind of like looking at it."

"I bet you'd like licking it more."

Laughter bubbles up in my chest...along with heat.

"Mmm," I murmur, dropping to one knee and then the other. I slide my hand along the outside of her thigh, lift it and settle it on my shoulder. "Maybe," I say, leaning in and flicking out my tongue, dragging the flat of it against her.

She shudders then demands, "More."

"Mmm," I murmur again, but this time I've buried my face in her pussy, so the sound vibrates through her, and I know she likes it because she squirms, grinding against me.

"More," she demands again.

"Hungry." I nip her flesh, suck at her clit, exploiting the spots I found the other night, taking my time this evening to find new ways to make her cry out my name, give voice to those demands. "Sexy." I slip my tongue inside her, cupping her ass so I can keep her close.

"Oh, God! Jace!" Her hips flex, riding my face, my tongue, and I feel it—the flutters of her pussy, the beginnings of her orgasm.

So I don't stop.

I use my tongue, my lips, my teeth. I use my fingers and body. I use—

Her hand in my hair flexes again, so tightly that pain

ripples through my scalp as she all but tears me away from that sweet cunt.

"Gorgeous," I warn.

Her eyes are hazy, filled to the brim with need. "Inside me."

Another demand, one that has me on my feet and spreading her legs wide around my hips, notching my cock at her entrance before I realize that I'm feeling all that slick heat directly on my dick, that I've almost plunged home without a—

"Condom," I gasp, exercising herculean control to not stroke deep.

The need in those emerald eyes increases a hundred fold. "Birth control shot," she rasps, rubbing herself against me. "And I was just tested a month ago. I haven't been with anyone but you," she adds, when my hands flex, holding her in place.

"Cookie."

"Just an FYI," she murmurs, half-slit eyes finding mine, pussy slowly soaking the tip of my dick. "Or we can find a condom."

I'm not even sure I have any condoms left.

We depleted my stash the other night.

"I'm tested regularly," I tell her.

"Good," she whispers.

"Good," I whisper back.

"Right." It's a murmur, those eyes staring at me expectantly.

For the life of me, I can't figure out why.

Probably because I'm lost in her beautiful face.

A hand on my jaw, her mouth curving lightly. "Okay, then."

"Okay, then," I repeat.

"Handsome," she says, "now's the time to fuck me."

My dick twitches, and all at once I'm aware of wet heat, of lush thighs, of this woman waiting for me...

To fuck her.

I shift and slide deep, making both of us groan.

It's...well, I've never had a woman without a condom before, so it's fucking incredible, tight and wet, hot and slick, internal muscles clasping and her moans ringing in my ears.

I want to go slow so I can savor it.

But slow quickly devolves to fast, to hard, to—

"Fuck!" she cries out, pussy clamping tightly around my cock.

And I'm right there with her, pumping rapidly, pleasure gathering at the base of my spine and then bursting outward, filling my entire body as my orgasm explodes out of me.

I keep us upright for a few seconds, then my legs give way and I slowly lower us to the floor.

"Fuck," she whispers long moments later, and at first, I think it's because of the same reason that word has been on repeat through my mind—fuck that was good, fuck I want to do that again, fuck how can I make my legs work so I *can* do that again.

Then she shifts, pushing lightly against my chest, lifting off me.

I lose the tight clasp of her cunt, the soft curves of her body, and I'm reeling from that, so I don't process what she's doing at first.

But eventually I see her crouched next to her pants, reaching into the pocket—

Pulling out her phone.

That's ringing.

She swipes a finger across the screen, lifts it to her ear. "Hey, boss." Her voice is slightly raspy as she says, "Yeah, no worries. I can be there in fifteen."

Fifteen minutes?

Or hours?

Because it'd better be fucking *hours.*

She hangs up the phone, sweat glistening on her naked skin, her breaths still coming a little short.

Then her eyes come to mine, and I don't miss the relief in the deep green depths.

Because now she can escape.

Goddammit.

"I'm leaving."

FIFTEEN

Marie

I'M REACHING for my underwear, thanking the universe for the perfectly timed interruption to my moment of insanity when I hear...

"Like hell you are."

I pause, mid untangle of my underwear from my leggings, and glance over at a scowling Jace. "Excuse me?" I ask, my tone bordering on dangerous.

"We just had that"—a nod toward the door, and I have the feeling that I'm not going to be able to look at those wooden planks of pleasure-bringers without thinking of Jace...and the pleasure *he's* brought me—"and you're just leaving?"

"I love my job." I manage to pull my underwear free and step into it, pulling the fabric up to my hips. I need to make a pitstop at the bathroom so I can clean up, but I'll do that far away from this dangerous man. "So, I need to go to the office."

I want him again.

Against the door, on the floor, in the bed—anywhere I can have him.

So, I have to leave.

"You have to work?"

I nod. "Yes."

And Angela Rosseau—my boss's horrible ex—has now given me the out I need. Never did I think that I would be thanking that awful woman for anything...but tonight the world has gone topsy turvy.

I start turning my leggings right side out, wrestling with the material, my hands shaking from an orgasm that nearly obliterated me. The task is arduous because I'm—and they're—so twisted up, but it doesn't take all my focus.

No matter how much I try to make that happen.

I hear him sigh softly as he pushes to his feet.

I hear his footsteps as he disappears down the hall.

Thank fuck he's not going to fight me on this.

I continue working on the fabric, turning the legs right side out and am just lifting my foot, readying to pull them on when Jace's hand slips around my waist. "Here, cookie."

My jump means that my back brushes against his front and combined with his hand on my middle, that phone call from Jean-Michel seems very far away.

Maybe I have time to—

"Here, gorgeous," he semi-repeats, and I glance down, my heart convulsing in my chest.

He's holding up a washcloth.

A *damp* washcloth.

Fuck. *Fuck.*

He brought me a washcloth so I can clean myself.

I...I can't with this.

Not his big, glorious dick. Not his strong body and teasing

words. Not him bringing me a cloth even though I'm leaving when he wants me to stay.

"What is this?" I whisper, even though I know.

Even though I can't handle something gentle, something sweet, something thoughtful...not like this.

Even though I really want him to lie and say it's something different.

That it means nothing.

Or maybe...that it means *everything*.

"You need to get to work, cookie," he reminds me.

"It was one time," I blurt.

"You've said that before." Still holding the washcloth, he bends, sweats hanging low on his hips and picks up his shirt, pulling it over his head.

"I have to get to the office."

"You said that too, gorgeous."

I did. On both counts.

So, I clamp my lips closed, reach for the cloth.

But he beats me to it, pushing the material of my underwear to the side and gently wiping away the evidence of our *only one time.*

And my traitorous heart pulses again.

Fucking hell.

Ignoring what that bit of care does to me, I yank up my leggings, not missing the heat in his eyes when my boobs bounce from me wrestling the fabric up my sweaty body.

He doesn't comment though—just passes me my bra top.

Which is even harder to wrestle on.

And he doesn't look away, those blazing hazel eyes locked on me.

I get lost in them, feel the heat begin to build in my belly.

At least until he turns away, releasing me from their hold. I scramble for my socks, pull them on, and am shoving my feet into my shoes when Jace crouches down beside me.

"Here," he says softly.

I look, careful to avoid those eyes this time.

But I can't avoid the sweatshirt he's holding out, the care he's extending again.

Christ, I can't take this.

"It'll be chilly tonight," he murmurs.

"I—"

He lifts and drops a shoulder in a careless shrug. "In case you don't have time to stop for a change of clothes."

"I—"

He doesn't reply, just pulls me up to my feet then tugs the sweatshirt over my head.

I'm immediately engulfed in the spicy male scent of him as the fabric drops over me, pooling beneath my butt, covering the top half of me in...*Jace.*

"I—" But I don't get more than that out.

I *can't.*

Because then Jace is touching my cheek with the backs of his knuckles. "Go kick some ass in the office, cookie."

He opens the door, and I start to step out into the hall, stopping when his lips come to my ear and his hand catches mine, "But I need you to know..."

I still, lungs catching, words forced out, "Know what?"

"That there will be more *one-times,* cookie."

Then he nudges me forward.

And closes the door to his condo.

SIXTEEN

Jace

MY ASSISTANT, Tom's, face tells me that my day is about to get longer.

And it's been pretty fucking long already.

How is it possible to have so many meetings in one day and still have an inbox that is out of control?

I encourage my employees to strive for a work-life balance, but I'm never more critically aware of how difficult that is in this day and age of cell phones and emails, Teams chats and conference calls than when I'm trying to find my own balance.

It's challenging to manage it all and I have a whole team managing *me* and my schedule.

"We have a problem," Tom says, which is not a surprise, considering the expression on his face.

"I've gathered that," I reply dryly, resisting the urge to wrench a hand through my hair.

I've been too busy to think about Marie—much, anyway— but it's been two days since she left my condo.

Two because she hasn't been in her place or the lobby or the gym—and yes, I kept my eyes peeled as I walked through the sunlit vestibule, as I ran on the treadmill and wished the one next to mine wasn't empty. I even jogged for a solid eight miles last night, staying in the gym far too late, hoping to catch a glimpse of bouncing brown curls as she strolled through the door.

There were no curls, no strolling.

Just me and my tired body and dick that was—is—desperate for more.

Unfortunately, it's also been two days since I've been inside her, since I've held and tasted her, since I gave her my hoodie with the complete and total intention to find a way to meet up with her and get it back, because shit is going down.

Our patent on a new blood clot removal device has been denied.

Because supposedly a competitor filed for it first.

A competitor that hasn't been in the clot removal business before.

Tell me how our decade of research and experience and trials has suddenly been bumped to the side for this unknown company with dubious roots.

Corporate espionage? Government shadiness?

Legit growth that we've somehow missed?

The last seems the least likely.

The first two—even though six months ago I would have said was insanity speaking—are possible.

But Genen-core is a relatively small company when it comes to big business.

I have five thousand employees and worldwide distribution of our products, with growth steady and exponential since COVID-times, but I'm not one of those huge tech billionaires.

We're in biomedical, a notoriously difficult field to make money, if only because of the length it takes to get products to market and the cost to properly conduct research and medical trials.

Because of that, our government contracts are critical, as are our relationships with insurance companies.

Something that I hated at first—I battled them far too often when I was caring for my mom.

Something I recognize as a necessary evil nowadays.

"What's happening?" I ask Tom, as he pauses in front of my desk, a sickly expression on his face.

"The FBI are here."

My brows fly up. "Want to run that by me again?"

He opens his mouth, but he doesn't get a chance to speak because the door to my office swings open, two women strolling inside, my assistant, Jo, chasing after them.

"I'm sorry, Mr. Henderson," she says. "They just—" She nibbles at the corner of her mouth, wincing.

"It's all good," I tell her. "Why don't you call it a day? I know you need to pick up Quinn from hockey practice." Her boy has recently picked up the sport, thanks to her NHL-playing boyfriend, West, and I know she treasures the time she gets to watch him.

She nibbles again, clearly torn between wanting to go hang out with her kiddo and her responsibilities here, especially when things haven't been going well today...or any of the last days.

And now the FBI.

So, with two FBI agents in my office, responsibility wins out in Jo's internal battle. "I can—"

"Go," I order softly. "Tom and the guys will be right behind you."

"I—" he begins to protest.

"You have that dinner with Matt tonight, remember?" I remind him. "You don't want to be late."

"I—"

I cut my eyes to Jo, thankful when she reads my unspoken words and comes over, taking Tom's arm.

"I'll get us out of here," she assures me.

I smile at her, inclining my head as she ushers Tom out.

I know it won't be long before the rest of the team is following suit.

The door to my office swings closed silently behind them.

I bite back a sigh and turn to the two agents. "How can I help you both?"

The woman whose tight brown curls remind me of Marie's steps forward, extending her hand toward me. "Athena Phillips—"

"Jackson," the woman, older with a tight blond bun corrects slyly.

"Agent Phillips," the first woman says dryly with a roll of her eyes. "Forgive my colleague. I'm a newlywed and Agent Robins thinks it's hilarious to remind me of that fact."

"Well, Agent Phillips—or Jackson," I add, earning a smile from the older woman. "How can I help you?"

"Sandra, please," she says, stepping forward and shaking my hand. "And we think it's best if we sit down and chat for a few minutes. Is now a good time?"

To sit down and "chat" with the FBI?

I have the feeling that it will never be a good time for whatever conversation is about to come my way.

But I round my desk and plunk down in my chair anyway.

I've never shied away from the hard shit.

And I'm not going to start now.

SEVENTEEN

Marie

"SO," Attie—excuse me, *Agent Phillips* asks. "Gonna clue me in on the sweatshirt?"

I roll my eyes at the other woman, but I know this is my own fault.

Once, I could have gotten away with wearing it, having rushed from home to the office (aka having rushed from Jace's place where he'd banged my brains out) to meet with her about Angela and her special brand of chaos.

But this is twice now.

"You're the one barging into my hotel room," I mutter, stepping back and holding the door wide enough for her to enter. "You don't get to critique my wardrobe choices."

"So says the woman who's always fabulously dressed who's now, all of a sudden, wearing *that*." She waves a hand along my body, from bottom to top, fuzzy socks to pajama pants to Jace's sweatshirt.

"Ah, now you're going to hurt my feelings."

"That being," she says without missing a beat, "a sweatshirt that decidedly seems to belong to"—her voice becomes a stage whisper—"a man."

I roll my eyes. "Stop messing around and tell me why you're here torturing me when you've already been torturing me at the office."

"I'll have you know," Attie says, "that I'm working overtime on this case for your boss—"

"You're working overtime for your husband," I correct.

"Who happens to be one of your boss's hockey players."

"Yes," I agree. "So we both benefit from putting this nonsense with Angela behind us—you get to solve your case and earn the undying love of your boy toy—"

"I already have it."

My heart squeezes at the confident words.

To have that, to know it with such assurance...

I can't lie—there's more than one thread of jealousy weaving through me.

"And," she goes on, "you get to have your boss less stressed because his ex is in jail like she should be and you can get back to doing your job as you prefer—without drama and sabotage."

I scowl.

"What?" she asks.

"I hate it when you talk sense."

Her mouth kicks up. "You love it, same as you'll love my update."

The last has me biting back the protest that was already welling up on my tongue.

Her smile grows. "Thought you'd like that."

"What's your update?"

Part of the craziness of the last weeks has revolved around Jean-Michel falling in love and being out of the office more. The rest is because we discovered that Angela was trying to con

Titan Capital employees into giving up confidential information (a thread that we shared with Attie and the FBI).

Angela, the ex from hell.

Angela, the absentee mom to Jean-Michel's daughter, Chrissy.

Angela, who took her absenteeism so far that she pretended she was dead.

Angela, who reappeared last year, tried to take half of everything, and then was spotted working with—or for, no one is really sure yet—the Lyon family, an East Coast crime conglomerate who've branched out to expand their smuggling and human trafficking business here to this side of the country.

I'm sure there's more, but I'm not privy to all the details of the investigation.

Angela seems to be both everywhere and nowhere, kicking up dust and chaos.

Working with lawyers and criminals alike.

But tonight, Attie tells me they're closing in.

The information passed along from our employee at Titan Capital is another layer, another piece of the puzzle.

"With any luck," Agent Phillips says after asking me to look into a couple of other contracts that connect with our biomedical partners, "we'll be wrapping this up in the next month or so and you can get back to controlling everything behind the scenes at Titan Capital."

"Not the wine," I quip, making a few notes in my laptop before saving and locking the screen. "I just drink it and leave the rest of the process to the powers that be."

"I knew I liked your style." She pushes up out of the chair, but when I expect her to head for the door, she just leans back against the dresser. "How long are you stuck here?"

"We're friendly enough to chat now?"

"Come now"—a wink—"you know we've been chatting from day one."

"Because you're pushy."

Another wink. "Because I know how to get the information I need."

"You know my condo flooded."

Because I was dragged out to dinner with Chrissy, Rory, and their hockey players, and Attie was dragged alongside me.

"I know, but I also heard you turning down offers to stay with the others left and right, and that"—she taps her temple—"piqued my spidey senses. There's more to the situation than a flood, and I think that it has something to do with that sweatshirt you're fondling."

I freeze, realize that I've been gently running my fingers over the hem of the sweatshirt, back and forth, back and forth.

Fuck.

I *am* fondling it.

I shove my hands into the pockets of my pants—lest I go back to fondling—and start for the door. "Goodnight, Attie," I say, mostly because I know calling her that instead of her preferred nickname of Ats drives her crazy.

"It's Ats," she corrects, right on cue, eyes narrowing slightly.

Victory is mine.

Ha!

Of course, it would be short-lived if she decided to do some scary ass karate shit to me as punishment for my teasing.

But she doesn't.

Instead, she trails me toward the door—albeit with a scowl.

FBI agents are scary.

"Ats," I find myself correcting, if only to make that scary look disappear, and reach for the handle. "I'll work on those files, get them over to you as soon as possible. And," I add lightly as I pull the door open, "I'll count down the days for Angela to receive her comeuppance."

A genuine smile, without—thankfully—a hint of murder. "Damn right you will." She pats my shoulder, but just before she steps through the door, she leans in and sniffs. "FYI, your sweatshirt smells like him."

I open my mouth to retort—something, *anything*.

But she's already gone.

EIGHTEEN

Jace

THE KNOCK on my door comes at literally the worst time ever.

The fucking FBI just left.

Outside my office is empty.

I've got an entirely new list of tasks I need to run by the legal department, files to pull, people to vet so I know who to trust.

I don't want to think that Jo or Tom or the others could be sabotaging my business...

But stranger things could happen—*have* happened.

So right now, I need to proceed with caution.

Proceed alone.

I glare at the door, shove my papers into my bag, at the same time calling out, "Come in."

I'm expecting it to be Tom or Jo circling back, here to get my ass home—hence me grabbing my bag and tossing it over my shoulder as the door cracks open. Save myself the argument about my work-life balance and all that. So, I'm not expecting to see—

"Brooks?" I ask on a frown.

"I see that you're thrilled to see me," he drawls, stepping inside and dropping a duffle bag by the door.

"What the fuck, man?" I round my desk, move over to him.

We hug, slapping each other's backs.

"Last I heard, you were living in France."

"Eh." He shrugs. "Got tired of feeling like a dumb American, so I decided that I needed to come stateside for a while."

I chuckle. "How long's that going to last this time?"

Another shrug. "Could be a week. Could be six months."

"Could be tomorrow," I quip.

He grins. "True. But I had my housekeeper stock my fridge, so I'm going to at least eat my way through Dolores's delicious food before I abandon the U.S. again."

"Oh good," I say dryly. "I can relax."

"Rude." He shakes his head, starts to turn for his bag. "I guess I'm not sharing her tiramisu with you."

I freeze. "She made tiramisu?"

"Not that it matters to you," he says, snagging the handles of his bag and hefting it up. "Since you're not going to eat any of it."

"I—"

He pulls open the door, steps out into the hall.

I grab my phone and wallet, my laptop and keys, and follow him.

Because if Dolores made tiramisu then she also made homemade pasta.

And I'm not fucking missing her homemade pasta.

Even if I have to break into his apartment.

He's waiting by the elevators, smirking at me.

"You're an asshole," I mutter, jabbing at the button he hasn't hit yet...because he knew I'd be right here.

Yes, I can be bribed through my stomach.

No, it's not that deep.

Plus, there's nothing more I'm going to accomplish here tonight. Even if part of me wants to tear through my laptop, file by file, until I discover once and for all if one of my employees is fucking over my business.

That's not only inefficient, I likely don't have the skills.

My background is in research, but of the medical nature. I'm more comfortable with microscopes than hard drives.

So, I need to consult legal. I need to give what they clear over to the FBI and let them conduct their forensic research, and I need to keep my eyes and ears open so that I can be helpful instead of a useless lump standing on the sidelines.

"Board problems?"

I blink, pulling myself out of my head, seeing that I followed him onto the elevator and we're heading down without me even realizing it. "No," I mutter.

"Production?"

I glance over at him. "What's with all the questions?"

"You're a million miles away and have a roadmap of scowl lines etched into your face"—he lifts and drops a shoulder—"it's either work that's giving you trouble, or..." His features sharpen, eyes locking onto mine. "Or it's a woman."

I jerk.

Then silently curse.

Because I've given away too much.

"Or it's both," he murmurs sneakily.

I jerk again.

Then sigh, knowing it's no use. Brooks has been my best friend since college. We waded through the shit for years before our companies took off, and he was there when my mom's health finally gave out and I lost her, inch by inch. And he didn't turn away from me when I couldn't handle it, spun out for probably far too long. Instead, he stuck by me, helped redirect my rage, and provided the initial capital to get Genencore off the ground.

And I was there when his wedding imploded and he was forced to walk away from the woman he loved.

In a few words, we've seen each other through the fucked-up realities of life.

And we've made it through to the other side while still remaining friends.

"Yeah," he says dryly. "It's both."

"Just leave it alone, yeah?"

He studies me for a few heartbeats then inclines his head. "I'll get it out of you after a couple of beers anyway."

He's not wrong, but I don't comment as the elevator doors slide open with a ding and we walk off, him trailing me toward my car. "I'm driving," I mutter.

Brooks just grins and says, "I call shotgun." He yanks at the passenger door handle and starts to climb in as he explains, "Had my Lyft drop me here and used my code to come up because I figured I'd have to tear you out of your office, you chronic over-worker."

Just the word Lyft has me pausing, thinking about a feisty brunette who's doing her level best to keep me at a distance.

Apparently for long enough that Brooks says,

"*Definitely* a woman."

I jump. Then scowl at my friend before tossing my bag into the back seat, where he's done the same with his duffle.

"And also probably work," he says. "Because it's always work."

My scowl deepens, and I flip him off as I drop into my own seat.

But I don't reply because he's also not wrong about that shit either.

Instead, I just start up the car and drive toward his building.

Tiramisu.

I need to focus on tiramisu.

NINETEEN

Marie

"MEOW!"

"Hold on, you demanding little fluff ball," I mutter as I carefully carry the food dishes across Chrissy's house and over to the ledge where her surly senior cat named Joan of Freaking Arc (yes, seriously) prefers to eat.

This being because the cat is old and surly...and has seen more rescue animals come through Chrissy's house than I've likely seen in my lifetime.

Jean-Michel's daughter runs a cat rescue.

His adopted in heart, but not on paper, daughter, Rory, runs a dog rescue.

Together, it's floof-tastic.

And while Chrissy has several rescue centers and her and Rory both have a team of foster parents and volunteers, every once in a while, I chip in to help with the fluff buckets.

Like when the hockey team that Jean-Michel owns, the Eagles, is on an extended road trip, taking the men, and this time—with me taking care of the pups and surly senior cat—the women too.

I don't mind.

I've got my work—my normal duties along with the material I pulled for Attie.

And I'm out of the hotel room for the next few days, days that should give the contractors enough time to put the final touches on my condo—finish up installing the floor and repainting the baseboards, doors, and walls.

The tile is installed. The vanity is repaired—along with the leak, I've been assured.

There's no avoiding the fact that I'll be moving home soon.

With Jace and his magnificent dick right down the hall.

I groan, shove that thought out of my head.

I'll just have to upgrade my vibrator.

Because I'm not going there again. I had my taste, it was glorious, and...now moving back to my regularly scheduled programing.

Plus, Joan and the sweet pups—Athena and Zeus—are good company.

Definitely much simpler company than whatever chaos Angela is orchestrating...and less confusing than my apparent inability to stay away from Jace.

My temple throbs and I shove that thought away.

Lots to do. Lots to distract myself with.

Joan's food on her perch. Two pups trailing after me as I prepare their meals. Then I'm working on feeding myself—or I start to pull out the ingredients I brought, but then stop and shake my head, a sigh escaping through my exasperated smile.

"Chrissy," I mutter, pulling out the container that has a sticky note with my name written on it.

I wouldn't let her pay me when her pet sitter got ill, so she and—I sigh again, shaking my head—Rory also, apparently, came up with an alternate form of payment.

Chicken pot pie.

And a huge, M&M-covered caramel apple.

My stomach rumbles and I pull both—along with a Diet Coke (not because I'm counting calories, but because I like the taste, okay?)—and set them on the counter. Then read the instructions on the note and turn on the oven.

I pop the pot pie onto a cookie sheet and slide it onto the rack (who needs preheating anyway?).

Then I put the puppers out of their misery and make their dinner, watching as they scarf it down in mere seconds before I take them into the back yard and let them do their bathroom business.

When we make it inside again, the timer is ready to go off, so I wash my hands, get a plate out and slice myself a salad, er, cut myself a chunk of the caramel apple.

Po-tay-toe. Po-tah-toe.

And then I'm diving into my food, a pair of pups laying on my legs, their begging eyes locked onto my fork during each and every trip it makes from my plate to my mouth. I don't cave on the chicken pot pie front, but I do give them an extra cookie after I've finished my chunk of candy-covered apple and wash the dishes.

As they chew, I snap some pictures of the critters, send them off to their respective owners, then the pups are in their crates and I'm bedding down in the guest room, a prickly Joan curled up at my feet.

She hisses at me, giving my legs a half-hearted swat as I settle in, but when I wake up, it's to find her curled against my hip.

I lay there, the sunshine of early morning streaming in through the windows, thinking that maybe I need to give in to all the cuteness that Rory and Chrissy trade in, and adopt a pet. Yeah, I travel a lot, but I could get a small dog, bring it with me like one of those fancy socialites. Or I could befriend a surly senior cat who prefers her solitude, hiring a pet sitter to check in regularly when I'm not home.

Either option would work.

I just don't know which is best yet.

Anyway, it'd be nice to not be alone every night.

And, since I'm not going to invite a man to share my bed, then it seems like a pet of some sort might be the best option.

Eventually, my cell buzzes, my alarm quietly chiming, and I snap out of my head.

Joan swats and hisses at me again as I climb out of bed, but her claws are sheathed, and I'm feeling the same streak of grumpiness, anyway. I'm liking the lazy morning, don't want to get out of bed.

Duty calls, though.

And with Jean-Michel gone, I need to hold down the fort.

So, I take care of pups and the senior cat. I make myself a light breakfast and pack the leftover apple and pot pie for my lunch. I do my makeup, put on my office casual, and then I go to work.

But all day long, I can't shake the feeling that a pet isn't going to fill the nagging loneliness inside me.

That only one thing can.

And it's also the one thing that I will never—*ever*—allow myself to have.

TWENTY

Jace

"AND THEN," I say after draining the dredges of my beer and setting the bottle onto the counter with a *clink*, "I wake up in the morning and the fucking woman is just gone. Gone!"

Brooks lips twitch and I don't refuse the fresh beer he passes over. "Women are complicated."

I scowl, something I've been doing a lot since Marie hijacked my Lyft. "They make things *unnecessarily* complicated," I mutter.

"This is true," he agrees, taking a swig of his own bottle.

"So, I've got the patent shit and a visit from the fucking FBI, and I know that the funds I finally got the board to earmark for the women's health division are going to be shifted away to handle the legal fallout of that shit, which means that we're not going to have enough data to launch the endometrioses treatment this year."

Brooks stills. "Fuck," he says. "Really?"

"Yup." I sigh, buzzed, but not buzzed enough to be optimistic. "And without the patent and the funds it will bring, we can't afford the funding for smaller trials. Which we need in order to go for FDA approval in the fourth quarter."

"Damn, that sucks." He nudges my foot with his. "Really. I'm sorry."

"I know you are."

"Is there anything I can do?"

"Have any ins with the FDA or patent office?"

He screws up his face. "Unfortunately, not. Security systems and biomedical haven't exactly formed the perfect crossover yet."

"What? Retinal scans don't require labs full of eyeballs?" I ask lightly, going for a lame joke.

Because lame is all I have right now—humor or otherwise.

Brooks throws me a pity chuckle, and then silence falls between us.

"I'll ask around," he says to break it. "Let you know if I hear anything helpful."

"Appreciated," I mutter.

The silence falls again.

And this time I'm the one to break it. "Do you..." My eyes cut to his and then away, focusing on the top of my bottle. "Do you think about her?"

I feel the tension in him like a punch to the gut, hard and intense and so strong it steals the breath from my lungs.

I expect him to tell me to fuck off, to shut up, to never talk about Briar, the woman he left at the altar, years ago now.

He grows quiet, stays that way for long enough that I think he's not going to answer.

But then he surprises the shit out of me by saying, "Yeah." A beat. "All the fucking time."

"I—"

He bumps my foot again, this time harder, his voice taking

on more urgency than I've ever heard from him before. "If she really means something to you, don't be a fucking moron like I was—"

"You said that you had to leave because—"

"I *thought* I had to," he says. "I even believed it at the time. But it was all bullshit, man."

"The threats weren't real?"

"No, the threats were there. Allowing them to drive us apart was the biggest mistake of my life. I could have done so many things differently, could have..." He closes his eyes, taps the top of the beer bottle against his forehead. "I could have made it work—kept her safe and not break her heart, kept her safe and loved her like she deserved." A long blip of quiet before he sighs and sets the bottle on the counter, eyes opening, gaze connecting with mine. "I didn't. And I lost her, which was fucking awful, but it's worse knowing I broke her—"

His voice cracks, eyes sliding from mine.

Fuck.

"Breakups are hard on both parties," I say, trying to soften the regret in every single line of his body. "I'm sure she's—"

"I visited her."

That has me sitting up straight in my stool, worry churning through my stomach. "You—"

"A couple years back. It was the anniversary of that day. I figured I'd find her out with her girlfriends, living it up." His voice drops. "Either that or married, having popped out the kids she wanted to so badly have."

"She didn't do either of those?"

A shake of his head. "No." The word sounds as though it was torn out of him. "She was sitting on her bed, her wedding dress laid out on the mattress beside her, and she was—" Another crack in that armor, the regret heavy in the words, the remorse spiking sharply through his eyes. "She was crying, man. She was holding it and crying, and I knew I fucked up. I knew I hurt her. But in that moment, I knew it was more than just hurt and tears. I *broke* her, and if we ever existed in a world where we could go back in time, I would go back and fix that, go back and make sure nothing ever touched her again—no matter the cost."

Christ, the thought of sweet personified Briar Ellis sitting on her bed, surrounded by her dress, *crying*...

I absently rub at the ache in my chest.

And I liked her, but I wasn't Brooks. I didn't love her, didn't worship her, didn't want to make her mine.

For my friend to have seen that...

I hate that for him.

For *them*.

"When something beautiful lands in your lap," he says, voice fierce now, eyes intense, grief tucked deep, deep down again, "don't fucking waste it."

"I won't," I promise him.

But even as the words cross my lips, I wonder if they're true. If I can really go there with Marie.

A heartbeat later, the memory of her sparkling green eyes, her bouncing brown curls, her razor-sharp wit flooding my mind...and I know I don't really have a choice in the matter.

The universe seems to have decided otherwise.

"So, you'll figure out a way to get your girl to stick around?" His smile is lame, approaching my lame attempt at a joke a few minutes ago.

I lean into that.

"Even if I have to handcuff us together."

"Kinky," he says on a chuckle that thankfully, almost sounds real.

I cling to that. "I learn from the master."

He rolls his eyes then changes the subject to the Eagles and how their season is going (spoiler alert: it's going much better since they fired their asshole of a head coach last year).

But even though the topic shifts and he turns back into my pain-in-the-ass best friend again, I don't forget what he told me.

And I promise myself that if the opportunity arises, I'm going to help him get Briar back.

TWENTY-ONE

Marie

PUPPY PATROL IS OVER.

Surly senior cat duty has finished.

And now I'm considering adopting two dogs and a gaggle of kittens and an adult cat who may or may not scratch me at every opportunity.

Because my condo is an empty shell that used to house something human (me) but now is just...empty.

New floors. For all intents and purposes, a new bathroom. And new baseboards and several new kitchen cabinets that weren't fixable, and new carpet in the bedroom. And...it's empty. Partly because my replacement furniture hasn't come yet, though it should show up in the next couple of days. But mostly because...

I'm alone.

I like being alone.

It's one of my favorite things—especially after having dealt with all the annoying people out in the world (and, day to day, I have to deal with a lot of them).

But tonight, alone feels wrong.

Hence the pet adoption.

A dog would get me out and walking. A cat would curl up on my lap as I sit on my nonexistent couch and watch a brain-rotting show about polygamists.

Both would soothe all sides of me, buffing away the sharp edges that poke at me, tell me to pay attention, fill in the dents and notches so that I'm complete.

But I don't think that would stop the persistent itchiness that exists just beneath my skin.

Because *that* prickly feeling is telling me to take a short trip down the hall, knock on a certain billionaire's door, and say, *"How about a three-peat?"*

He'd be down.

Unless he's already moved on and—

"Ugh," I groan, that thought hitting hard enough to hurt. *"Enough."*

I've lost my freaking mind. If he moved on to another woman that's a good thing. I told him once and it was twice, that's bad enough. Better that he scratch his itches with another woman. Then I won't get attached and do something stupid.

And is that why you're still wearing his sweatshirt?

God, why does the logical bitch inside me have to be so fucking *logical?*

Because I know that even *I*—logical side or not—don't believe the lie I've been trying to tell myself—that it's comfortable, and that's the only reason I've worn the hoodie every night.

Comfort isn't why I haven't washed it.

Comfort isn't why I inhale deeply every time I pull it over my head.

But my stubborn side doesn't want to give in to the logical bitch, so I move down the hall, rolling my suitcase alongside me, not stopping until it's on that new carpet and I'm unzipping it. I put my toiletries away then start in on my clothes—hanging my work outfits that can be reworn, putting the rest in the dry cleaning section I've designated in my hamper, splitting the other dirties into darks and lights.

I turn to leave, reality TV and wine imminent.

But I stop on the threshold.

Then my stubbornness ramps again, and I pull off Jace's sweatshirt, shoving it into the dark hamper compartment.

I'll wash it and leave it at his door.

Then this will be done.

Nodding to myself, I snag my pillows and comforter off the bed, carry the load into the front room where my only TV in the apartment is hooked up and working (because I had it mounted to the wall before Floodgate 3000). Then I set about making a little nest for myself.

It requires a second trip with blankets before it's comfortable enough for proper trash TV viewing.

And then I'm on snack prep—opening a bottle of wine, cutting some hunks of cheese and bread, putting them together with some honeycomb from the farmer's market near Chrissy's house and the leftover slices of my caramel apple.

Not the fanciest charcuterie board.

But a delicious one.

I settle it on my blanket and pillow nest, thinking that the no pet thing isn't the worst right now—considering that I don't have to guard my snacks against pilfering pooches—and I'm going back for the glass of wine when there's a knock at the door.

My gaze goes to my snacks longingly.

If it's Chrissy and Rory—not unlikely considering they've

both been demanding to tour my place and also because they're worried about me not having any furniture except for my bed (which only survived because the legs on the frame are metal and high, situating my mattress and linens above the flood).

I've been putting them off because they're busy and Chrissy's pregnant and they were traveling.

But it wouldn't be a surprise if they've finally run out of patience.

I groan softly but move to the door when the second knock comes. If it *is* them, they won't give up with a simple knock or two. They'll stand outside and call my bluff, not budging until I let them inside and give them the full tour of my empty condo.

My fingers wrap around the handle and I twist. "You may be here," I say as I pull the door open, "but I'm not sharing my snacks."

I should have realized Chrissy and Rory couldn't make it to this floor without buzzing up.

I *should* have looked through the fucking peephole.

But I didn't.

So, when the door's fully open, revealing none other than sexy, yummy-penis-wielding Jace Henderson, I'm momentarily frozen in place.

Gorgeous.

Tall.

Strong.

Smells like heaven...

And smiles like sin.

"That's fine, cookie," he says, lifting an arm and showing me he's holding a bag. "I bought my own."

And then he waltzes right inside.

TWENTY-TWO

Jace

FUCK, I want to kiss the befuddled look off her face.

But Brooks's words have been running through my head nonstop since we spent the evening together.

So, when I got the text from security telling me that Marie was back—and with a suitcase in hand—I didn't hesitate. I closed down my computer, made a couple of key stops, and then headed straight home. Or well, straight *here*.

"You sure you don't want to share your snacks, gorgeous?" I ask as I set the bag on the counter and start pulling out what I brought. "I think you might change your mind."

She doesn't reply right away, and I chance a look up, see that she's staring at the open door like it's grown a second head.

Then she seems to shake herself, shutting the door and turning to face me.

Turning to *glare* at me.

"What are you doing here?"

"You're officially moving back in?" It's a question, but one I already know the answer to—mostly because I signed off on the invoice for the work today.

There's a long pause.

Then she sighs. "Yeah," she mutters.

"Smells like paint." I don't like that, don't like that she might be exposed to the fumes, that she might hurt herself.

Something crosses her face—like she sees the thoughts running through my mind, as though she knows I don't like it. But all she says is, "I opened a window and it's better already."

I inhale, trying to test that for myself.

Then I weigh whether or not I can convince her to come down the hall and stay at my place, where there aren't any fumes.

Then I stifle a snort.

Yeah, like I'm going to win that battle.

So, I turn back to my bag, pull out the rest of my food.

It's nothing fancy, not expensive, just good quality pastries from Molly's bakery, some wine that a work colleague gave me, and some—

"Ramen?"

The word is filled with awe, said softly, but close to me, right near my ear.

Victory bubbles up in my chest.

She likes ramen. Fuck, yeah. Does a large portion of the world also love the dish? Well, yes. But *Marie* clearly likes it and I brought it, so I may as well have climbed Mt. Everest."

"You changed your mind then?"

Her brows drag together, one unruly curl escaping and curling over her cheek. "About what?"

"About sharing your snacks."

Her face relaxes, eyes flicking to the side. I follow her gaze, see the plate balanced on top of a pile of pillows and blankets.

Cheese and bread and—thank God, I stopped for pastries—an apple covered in caramel and M&Ms.

My girl has a sweet tooth.

Well, I have something for that too.

"I don't know," she says, never backing down from the challenge. "My cheese is really good and that's the last of my apple." A lazy shrug. "Plus, the bread is freshly baked from Molly's."

"Well"—I reach for the brown bag—"these are freshly baked from Molly's *and* they have apples." I pull out the trio of apple cinnamon muffins. They're still warm, from one of the last batches of the day, and my stomach rumbles when my nose catches wind of the spicy scent.

"Are those apple cinnamon muffins?" It's a greedy question and a bolt of triumph shoots through me.

I nod, break off a piece, and shove it into my mouth, moaning when the flavor explodes on my tongue. "Sure is," I say once I've chewed and swallowed. "What's that worth to you?"

"A blow job."

I choke on the second bite I'd shoved into my mouth, coughing as I try to clear my throat.

And not missing that her expression becomes triumphant.

That feeling is going around—too bad hers is because I'm slowly dying due to a delicious baked good.

"Drink," she murmurs a few moments later, taking pity on me and setting a wine glass in front of my hand.

I scoop up the glass, guzzle back the wine, knowing that it's a good one, but unable to enjoy it.

Because...still slowly dying.

"You know, if you choke to death in my kitchen, the blow job is off the table."

I start coughing anew, but I do it glaring at her. "So...not...helping," I manage to rasp out when my throat begins to relax.

"You're the one who barged into my home," she says sweetly.

"So you don't want the ramen?"

Her eyes narrow and then she leans down and considers the label, snagging the one with the egg and pork broth—so noted. "Saving your life with the glass of wine is more than a tradeoff for ramen."

"Are we ignoring the fact that you made me choke in the first place?"

"Are you really that much of a prude between the sheets that talk of a blow job scandalizes you?"

I snake out an arm, draw her flush against me. "I think you know exactly *who* I am between the sheets, cookie."

Her lips part, and I feel it then, the way her body melts against mine, the siren's call of her desire, the memories of naked skin and lush curves and slick, *slick* heat.

But I didn't come here for this.

I don't just want a quick orgasm and to watch her curls bounce as she disappears out the door—or sends me packing.

I want more.

I want to know who she is beneath the confident, stubborn, gorgeous façade.

So, when her lips part, silently inviting me to taste, and her body melts further, plastering all those soft curves against me, I don't accept the silent invitation, don't take what's so clearly being offered.

Instead, I tamp down the need coiled tight in my belly.

When something beautiful lands in your lap, don't fucking waste it.

I'm not going to.

Not today.
Not ever.

TWENTY-THREE

Marie

I'M in Jace's arms again.

And I can't bring myself to care.

Because he's big and strong and hard—*everywhere*.

I shift a little closer, arching up, not caring about muffins and ramen or cheese and wine.

He's better.

The fire we create is better.

He bends down, and I shift closer, readying myself for—

The kiss on the forehead.

What the fuck?

I blink once, twice, but that doesn't change anything, and it doesn't bring his lips to mine. Worse, it gives him time to drop his arms and *step away*.

What the *actual* fuck?

He starts opening cabinets, not stopping until he finds the ones with my dinnerware, pulling out two bowls and a plate, setting them on the island by the food he brought. Then he goes back to making himself at home in my kitchen, opening drawers until he locates the silverware. Forks and two pairs of chopsticks join the pile.

What is going on here? And why do I suddenly feel as though I'm in far over my head?

Probably because I am.

He arranges the muffins and—sweet baby Jesus—he also brought Molly's peanut butter chocolate chip cookies. Two of them that are almost the size of my head.

My skinny jeans are going to protest.

He pours broth in the takeout containers, makes several trips over to my blanket and pillow pile, and...I just watch him.

It's when he's on his last trip—this time with both hands full carrying our wine glasses and the bottle of wine I'd opened earlier—that I finally unstick.

"What the hell are you doing?"

He picks up the remote, turns on the TV, making himself at home by turning on the Eagles' game.

I stomp over, snatch it from him.

"I don't like hockey," I mutter. Unless it involves an owner's box and free snacks, I think. But I keep that sentiment to myself before I add, "And if you're invading my relaxing night at home then you're going to watch what I want to watch and not complain about it."

I expect him to argue.

Instead, he shrugs. "It's your night and your condo." Then he picks up his bowl and chopsticks and gets to work on the ramen.

Which reminds me.

Ramen.

I hit the streaming service, load up my episode, and hit play.

Then get to work on *my* ramen.

This is so much better than bread and cheese and caramel apple slices—and that half-assed charcuterie board was damned good to begin with. Now, my belly is filled with tender noodles, succulent meat, spicy, hearty sauce...and *then* I get to chase it with cheese, bread, wine, apples, muffins, *and* half of the peanut butter chocolate chip cookie.

I want to finish the rest of it.

But my belly is full to bursting.

Still, I look at it longingly as I set it back onto the plate in front of me.

Jace, who's been watching the show with all the intensity of a man studying a bug beneath a microscope, turns to me and chuckles.

He didn't make as much progress on his ramen—or his cookie.

But I'm suitably impressed that he both chose so well and that he consumed the goodies with equal abandon. Usually guys like him are all—my body is my temple and shit. And I can't be with a man who can't sit in front of the TV and chow down every once in a while.

And *that's* a dangerous thought to allow to cross my mind.

I'm not going to *be* with any man. Not today. Not ever.

And yet you're cuddled up on the floor next to him, watching your favorite show, so what does that say?

Ugh. The logical side of my brain seriously needs to fuck all the way off.

"What?" I ask grumpily because I despise the mental circles I've been going through. Meanwhile, the man is just sitting there without a care in the world. Chuckling.

And staring at me like I'm said bug under said microscope.

His gaze flicks from the half-eaten cookie up to mine. "I'm just enjoying the consternation on your face at not finishing that." He tugs at one of my curls and emotions slide through my middle at the tender action. I don't...well, I don't know what to do with them—the emotions *or* the tenderness. "I'm impressed, cookie," he says. "But remind me to never take you on in an eating contest."

"Is that why you call me *cookie?*" I ask suddenly.

Maybe he'd noticed me downing the free—and delicious—food at the gala. They'd had platters and platters of cookies from Molly's. So many, in fact, that I had contemplated stuffing some in my purse to take home.

Alas, my handbag wasn't big enough.

I would have ended up with just crumbs.

His lips twitch. "No, gorgeous."

"Then why?" I press.

He tilts his head from side to side, studying me intently. "I had a dog named Cookie." One shoulder lifts, drops. "You remind me of her."

"I-I remind you of a *dog?*" I sputter.

"Yup." A beat. "Her coat was the same color as your hair."

It takes me a second to realize it—the man is teasing me.

And I don't know how to process that either. His eyes are dancing, but his words aren't a pointed comment about me eating too much or that I need to fix my hair. It's like he's actually impressed, like he actually is into my crazy mass of curls... and is that something men are with women like me?

Not normally.

And...more mental circles. I've got a tornado happening in there now.

"I like to eat," I mutter. "And genetics gave me the hair."

"And Cookie too." His mouth kicks up. "But I like to eat, gorgeous, so I'm just glad you enjoy something I do." He picks up a slice of apple, starts munching on it. "Though, I can't say that extends to TV." A jerk of his chin toward the screen. "You can't seriously watch this, can you?"

"I'll have you know that I'm fully aware that trash TV is trash TV."

He finishes the apple slice, sips on his wine. "What about it appeals to you?"

Maybe I could brush that off as a judgmental question if he didn't look so earnest.

But it's like he's actually interested in my answer.

So, I don't dismiss him with a quip. Instead, I stop, ponder that. It's not something I've thought about all that much. "It's an escape, I guess," I say quietly. "I love my job, but it's stressful and involves a lot of travel. Sometimes it's nice to just turn off my brain for a while and watch people act like idiots on TV."

He considers the screen for a long moment. "Well, you certainly have the idiot part right."

"Excuse me, sir," I mock grumble. "They're not *all* idiots."

"I'll remind you that you were the one using the term."

"I said *acting* like idiots, not that they are them." Though, to be fair, some of my favorite reality TV personalities *are* idiots.

"Touché," he murmurs. "So, it's the escapism," he goes on before I can press my point further. I get that. Though, my preferred mode of escaping reality is through sports." He snags the remote, points it at the screen, bringing the feed of the Eagles' game back up.

"I—"

Another click has it swinging back to my show, cutting off my protest.

He tugs my errant curl again. "Just checking the score."

I'm so undone by that touch, by his closeness, by the fact that he *turned* it back, that I forget myself for a moment.

And I reveal too much.

"Ugh, hockey." I set the remote carefully out of his reach. Something he clocks, if the way his mouth curves up is any indication. "Between you and Jean-Michel, I can never get away from this crap."

He's still.

Then he slowly turns to face me, and there's something in his eyes that I can't read.

Something that has my heart thudding against my rib cage, that has my pulse speeding through my veins, that has me wanting to rewind the moment and take it back.

Because I've given Jace Henderson a piece of me.

And I may never be able to get it back.

"As in Jean-Michel Dubois?"

TWENTY-FOUR

Jace

JEALOUSY TEARS THROUGH ME.

Hot and red and devastating.

Brooks is right. Losing someone like Marie...it would fucking kill.

And losing her to a man like Jean-Michel Dubois? A good man, a protective man, a man who doesn't fuck around with those who he claims as his?

That would be a thousand times worse.

The bottle of Oak Ridge wine on the counter—delicious when I drank it, but now churning in my stomach like battery acid.

The expensive condo.

The nice clothes.

The charity event.

She's connected to the multibillionaire, and I have the feeling it's not going to be in a way I enjoy, given the edgy expression that creeps onto her face. "Yes," she says quietly. "Jean-Michel Dubois."

Fucking hell.

"How do you know him?"

She pauses, head tilting to the side, emerald eyes studying mine, challenge in their depths, as though she already knows the answer. "How do *you* know him?"

"He's a colleague."

More studying, eyes locked on mine. Then she says quietly, "Jean-Michel is my boss."

Relief and jealousy war inside me.

Relief because she's not his when I'm desperate to make her mine.

Jealousy because he gets to work with her, gets to know her, and I'm...struggling to pick up the barest threads of what makes Marie...*Marie.*

"Oh," I say. "So you work at Titan Capital?"

"I'm on his executive team. I started as his assistant but now oversee most of the corporate division."

Jean-Michel is not just her boss.

She's an extension of him, a face of the company, his right hand.

And considering how important Tom and Jo are to me, I know that I can't overstate Marie's value to him.

Which means...

I'm likely going to have a pissed off, protective billionaire on my ass if I keep pursuing her.

Something that would have been a huge turnoff for any other woman.

Something that barely has me batting an eye before I say, "Tell me about it."

She stills, wine glass in hand. "Tell you about it?"

"Yeah, cookie. Clearly your job is important to you—"

She opens her mouth, eyes flashing with annoyance.

"—and I don't say that like it's a bad thing," I quickly tack on. "I love what I do too. But I know a little about business and *overseeing the corporate division* doesn't sound like an easy job."

"It isn't."

"So"—I give in to the urge and tug at a curl again—"tell me about it."

"You can't possibly want to hear about conference calls or Teams meetings."

"God, no." My lips twitch. "I get enough of them on a daily basis."

"I bet you do, Mr. CEO of Genen-core."

My smile widens. "So I'm the only one who wasn't paying attention?"

"You've been in newspapers and blog posts." She takes a sip of her wine. "And I, for one, actually read the name tags at fundraisers."

I wince. "In fairness to me, glancing at a woman's name tag often puts me in dangerous territory."

She grins then orders, "Explain."

"Because you all attach them"—I wave a hand toward her chest—"you know…"

"I don't know." Dancing emerald eyes. "Maybe you can elaborate on that?"

"Elaborate?" I shake my head, lips twitching.

"Yes. Or maybe enumerate the various other places a name tag should go."

"Elaborate and enumerate. Man, you must really get paid the big bucks using words like that."

She swats at my chest. "It's not like I'm talking about your ubiquitous predilection for a certain female body part."

"I think you mean my obsession with your tits," I stage

whisper, feeling a hundred feet tall when she tosses her head back and laughs.

Then she drops her chin back down, eyes connecting with mine. "For the record, there's nothing stopping you from furthering your obsession, handsome."

I go hard.

One sentence. Hot eyes.

And I want to fuck her.

She'd let me. I could strip her naked on this pile of pillows and blankets, fuck her with fingers and tongue and dick. But the night wouldn't end the way I want—she'd either kick me out before she went to bed or I'd find myself alone in the morning again, her apartment or not.

"That's not what tonight is about."

Worry creeps into her expression, but her words are light. "Okay, you can table your obsession and try your hand at making me come instead."

My cock goes even harder.

Fucking hell, this woman will be the death of me.

"Or," I say slowly, "you can tell me where you learned such big words."

She laughs.

"Either that or fill me in on these"—I jut my chin toward the TV, where the show has been playing even though neither of us are really paying it much mind—"characters and why they think finding a third so they can form a throuple, when their relationship is pretty much in tatters without the complication of adding a third person, is a good thing."

"Because they want to up their OnlyFans subscribers." A shrug. "Either that or they're truly delusional. It really could go either way."

I grin. "And the big words?"

"I went to college, handsome. I thought for a heartbeat that

I wanted to be an author. Turns out"—she glances over at me, the edges of her mouth curving up—"I much rather enjoyed reading books than attempting to write them."

"What do you like to read?" I ask...and it's too fast, too intense, too *interested* in the answer.

Those emerald eyes hold mine again, seeing that, seeing too much.

Something that's proven by her answer. "The same thing as everyone else."

Laughter bubbles up in my chest. "You know that there are about a hundred different genres of books, right?"

"Yes." She glares. "I was given that lesson at the same place I learned the fancy words."

"And I noticed you haven't mentioned the smutty novel I caught you devouring the other day."

"*I* noticed you didn't mention if you could even read in the first place."

I tug at a curl. "Always so sassy."

"Always trying to piss me off."

"That's because you're beautiful all the time, but most especially when you're pissed."

Her eyes go wide, plump lips parting in surprise, and I decide to take advantage of her befuddlement this time, leaning close and slanting my mouth over hers.

Sparks instantly.

Heat and desire and...quickly fraying control.

"Come to dinner with me," I murmur as I pull back, both of our lungs working hard, our breaths mingling.

Soft and melty transforming into cold flecks of emerald in a mere heartbeat.

She pushes at my chest, shifting back at the same time. "I don't do relationships, remember?"

"Yeah, about that," I say. "Why not?"

"Because all men are assholes who push and take advantage and who, deep down, hate women so will do anything in their power to subjugate them."

I admit that the intense words take me by surprise.

She presses her advantage—scooping up the plates and glasses, carrying them to the kitchen, setting them with a series of alarming clatters into the sink.

I take my time climbing to my feet and following her.

"You don't believe that," I say softly.

Her shoulders go stiff then she slants a glare at me over her shoulder. "Now you're going to mansplain to me what I believe?"

A dangerous question.

"I don't have to," I tell her. "Because you work for Jean-Michel Dubois. Which means that you've met a good man, and I know him—though not as well as you do, I'm sure. But I also know there are more good men at Titan Capital, on the Eagles' roster. So, there must be more good men you've encountered." A beat as her face changes. "Because Jean-Michel wouldn't accept anything less."

I've met the powerful businessman, had tense meetings with him.

But there's one thing that never changes—his moral code.

It can be annoying as fuck, that high standard tough to match.

But I've always respected it.

And I like that Marie's work life is surrounded by it.

She huffs out a sigh, turning her back on me and cranking on the sink.

Which tells me that she knows I'm right.

Which...has the devil in me making a reappearance, prodding the bear, just a little.

"You're scared."

She goes still again. Then slowly spins to face me. "Excuse me?"

An even deadlier question.

"You're scared to go to dinner with me." I step closer. "Because you might find that you like me."

Her eyes flash. "You're a real asshole, you know that?"

"Bawk."

She jerks. "What—?"

"Bawk. Bawk. *Bawk.*"

"Are you being serious right now?"

"About you being chicken?" I grin lazily. "Damn right."

"I'm not—"

"Bawk. Bawk. Bawk!"

"Jace."

"Bawk!"

Her mouth clamps closed.

"Bawk."

"You're a child—"

"Bawk. Bawk."

"And—"

"Bawk."

"Ugh!" She tosses her hands up. "Fine. You really want to torture yourself by sitting across a table from me and buying me a meal? Great!"

"Great," I repeat. "Dean's. Seven o'clock tomorrow night."

"I'll order the most expensive shit on the menu," she warns.

I shrug. "I have plenty of money."

"I'll—"

"Don't go back to finding excuses and chickening out now, cookie."

Her mouth drops open and I take advantage, stealing a short, hot kiss.

Then I take my victory and get the hell out of there.

Though, I can't resist calling, "Seven. Dean's," just before the door shuts behind me.

I don't miss the *thunk* that tells me something very heavy was thrown at it a mere heartbeat after my exit.

I'm grinning as I walk down the hall to my condo.

And I dream of brown curls, soft smiles, and emerald eyes.

Mine.

TWENTY-FIVE

Marie

I'VE BEEN a wreck all day long.

Jumpy. Off-kilter.

Forgetful.

The only good thing is that Jean-Michel is out of town.

So, he wasn't there to witness my failings...and then press me into spilling my guts.

I'm sure he'll hear about it.

Attie had sure looked at me sideways during our brief meeting—I'd pulled together some additional material for her and her team—but the case with Angela was heating up so rapidly that, luckily for me, she was too busy to really interrogate me.

Likely, that will come soon enough.

And likely, none of those will come soon enough to get me out of this date.

I thought about blowing it off, disappearing to a hotel again, maybe scheduling an emergency business trip to take care of something extraneous and unimportant...but something that needed to be taken care of in a time zone far, far away.

But Jace will just be here when I get home.

Ready to pounce...or maybe goad me into losing my temper and agreeing to a wholly stupid date.

Sex is easy.

Dates are...not.

They lead to me being an idiot.

"And you're not being an idiot right now?" I ask my reflection.

Because even though it would make the most sense to put on my ugliest, frumpiest dress, to slap on my makeup in the most unflattering way...something stopped me.

Or maybe, something egged me on.

To pull out my sexiest little black dress, my skimpiest lingerie to wear beneath it, my strappy silver sandals.

So maybe, I'm determined to torture him—and also myself, imagining his reaction to the various parts of my outfit.

Or maybe, I just want him to think I'm beautiful.

That thought has alarm bells blaring through my head, has the reality of what I'm doing, what I'm playing with ricocheting across my mind.

The tornado inside my brain has become an F5.

I'm spinning out, caught in the dangerous crosshairs, debris flying my way.

"I can't do this," I hiss at my reflection, reaching for my makeup wipes.

But before I can open the package, there's a knock at the door.

"Shit," I whisper, freezing, wondering if whoever is on the other side—likely a certain troublesome billionaire—is going to go away.

My answer comes approximately ten seconds later...

With another knock.

I look around my bathroom like an escape hatch is suddenly going to open up—and when, spoiler alert, it *doesn't*, I glare at my reflection.

Too much boobage.

Too much leg.

Too...just *much*.

But there's another flipping knock and—

"Open up, cookie!" Jace hollers through the wood. "I can hear the trashy show playing on the TV and know you're in there."

"Dammit," I whisper.

I should have put my earbuds in and blasted a podcast, then I could have legitimately ignored the knocking.

Unfortunately, I can't.

Because it keeps coming.

And it's just us on this floor. The man can knock till his heart's content and not disturb anyone—or anyone aside from me.

So, I know I just need to get this over with.

I scowl at the clock as I walk to the door, noting that the annoying man is fifteen minutes early, probably—rightfully— assuming that I'd be freaking the fuck out and pulling the plug on this shit right about...well, ninety seconds ago.

It's that annoying thought paired with the still annoying knocking that has my scowl deepening, my focus not on checking the peephole.

But on giving Jace Henderson a piece of my mind.

Except, the sharp retort doesn't escape the tip of my tongue.

Because I'm swallowing it, my mouth dropping open, heat boiling in my belly, sending a flush over me from head to toe.

Jace just smiles sexily at me. "Hey there, gorgeous."

More heat, liquid desire gathering between my thighs, my nipples tightening when his gaze leaves my face, trails oh so slowly down my body.

And then I'm being proverbially reduced to ash.

Because I get to see the way his face changes as his stare traces over my body...

I don't think I've ever seen something so breathtaking.

"Gorgeous," he repeats softly, stepping forward and gently touching my cheek.

We stand there, close together, silence stretching, staring into each other's eyes. I'm studying the golden flecks in those hazel irises, mixing with the green and brown. They look different today, more green and I think it's because of the hints of emerald in his shirt.

A shirt I can only see a small triangle of.

Because the rest of his body is clad in a suit that is fitted to such absolute perfection that even the most celibate people on the planet would line up to get a look.

He's strong, his frame powerful—something I knew from that night in the gym, from the naked horizontal (and otherwise) time I spent with his body. And it's not like I haven't seen him in a suit before—that night of the fundraiser, several times here in the building.

But this suit is different.

Or maybe it's that *I'm* different.

Something that has alarm rippling through me—alarm that doesn't have a chance to take charge and erect even stronger barriers against this man because he's stepping toward me, those fingers trailing down my cheek, running lightly over the edge of my jaw. Then he shifts slightly and I hear a crinkle and—

My heart rolls over in my chest.

"These are for you."

Maybe I'd expect flowers, especially on a first date, but my nose tells me differently even before he unrolls the top of the bag, revealing—

Molly's peanut butter chocolate chip cookies.

Another hard pulse of my heart, the organ launching itself against my ribs.

"Jace—"

He steps by me and brings the bag to the counter in the kitchen, carefully rolling the top back down so the goodies stay fresh.

The suit that fits him like sin.

The cookies he brought because he knows I like them.

The careful preservation by gently rolling the bag back down...

I know I'm in trouble.

Because all my plans of telling him this date is off, to go home and leave me to my reality TV because we are never—*ever*—going to happen fly right out of my head.

"Grab your purse, cookie," he orders softly.

And I don't even resist.

I just grab my phone and purse, let him help me into my coat, and I...

Follow him right out the door.

TWENTY-SIX

Jace

"RIGHT THIS WAY," the hostess murmurs, and I don't miss the hungry look she tosses my way before she turns and starts leading us to the private table I'd arranged for in the back of Dean's.

The steakhouse is a city classic—fifty-plus years in the business and reservations are still nearly impossible to get.

Luckily, I know Dean himself.

And he did me a solid, arranging for the table.

I know it's because he's a nosy fuck, same as I know that Brooks will likely text me later because I made the mistake of telling him I couldn't meet up tonight.

And then when he asked why I couldn't, I'd made a second mistake in telling him the real reason why.

So, now I have two nosy fucks on my case.

And a woman who doesn't want to be here.

I step forward and take her coat, passing it to the hostess before I tug out her chair.

Flowers and woman, lush curves and silken skin.

She sits and I push it in, unable to resist trailing my fingertips down the bared flesh of her spine revealed by her dress.

I don't miss her shiver, but I rein myself in before I stroke again, rounding the table, passing off my coat as well, and settling into my own chair.

She's beautiful, so fucking beautiful it takes my breath away.

And that's why I don't realize I'm staring at her, not speaking.

At least until she whispers, "Why are you looking at me like that?"

"You know why," I say softly, but the genuine confusion on her face has me adding, "You knew exactly what that dress was going to do to me, cookie."

Confusion slides away, replaced by mischief.

Fucking beautiful, that.

"See, gorgeous?" I tease, leaning forward and running the backs of my knuckles along the bare skin of her arm, watching the goose bumps appear, seeing the way my touch has her melting.

She may not want anything serious—or cough, anything more than a quick fuck before I walk my ass out the door—but she likes my touch and hasn't had her fill and so...I'm going to take advantage of that, going to bind her to me, going to make her mine.

And then what happens?

The question is quiet, silky smooth, but with a hidden barbed edge.

Because...*then what?*

Because what if—

"I don't know what you're talking about." Her chin lifts, but the mischief doesn't disappear. A good fucking thing too because it snaps me out of the bullshit in my head.

"You don't?" I let my hand continue trailing down, brushing our fingers together, loving the way she shivers.

And I'm not enough of a gentleman to miss that the hard peaks of her nipples are pressing against the fabric of her dress.

"Are you cold?" I ask pointedly.

Her eyes narrow, and she jerks her hand back, mouth opening, but before whatever razor-sharp response she's come up with can shoot off the tip of her tongue, I hear,

"Jace!"

I glance to the side and hop to my feet. "Dean," I grin, shaking his hand when he extends it toward me and then dropping my voice to murmur for his ears only, "Thanks for this."

He leans back, winks. "You owe me one." Then he's rotating toward Marie, turning on the Italian charm. "And who is this beautiful creature?"

Creature?

Shit.

I brace for explosion—or at least for Marie's trademark sass. I already owe Dean one for literally creating a table for us tonight in his already full restaurant. I don't really want to have to come up with another form of repayment—or a dozen because when Marie gets going, she *really* gets going.

But my bracing and the potential interjections that fill my brain in the split second after Dean's question aren't needed.

Marie blushes.

Actually blushes, pink spreading prettily on her cheeks.

"I'm Marie," she murmurs, lifting her hand and then—what the actual fuck?—*not* socking Dean in the face when he lifts it to his lips and presses a kiss to the back of it.

"Lovely to meet you," he says, "and may I just say that your perfume is intoxicating?"

The fucker, especially the way he lingers close to her, inhaling.

I jerk forward, just barely stopping myself from ripping his arm away from her.

I don't care that Dean is sixty if he's a day. If he doesn't stop touching her, I swear to fuck I'll—

He drops his arm and, thankfully, my blood pressure follows suit, head and temper clearing enough so I don't have to be the one at fault for repaying Dean those dozen favors. "This man"—a jerk of his head toward me—"never brings women here—"

Yeah, because I've never been this obsessed with one.

"—so you must be really special."

Fuck. She is. But also, I basically goaded her into the date because she's so gun shy. I don't need Dean running her off.

"Oh," Marie says, her gaze flicking to mine, but only for a heartbeat. Then it goes back to Dean's, and I'm left wondering if the flicker of softness I saw in those emerald depths was real... or if I'm so pathetic that I imagined it.

I don't get the chance to sit in that.

Because Dean's still talking.

"What do you like to eat, *amore?*"

She nibbles at the corner of her mouth, expression turning shy. "Anything."

"Tsk, tsk," he says. "There has to be a favorite."

"Really, anything is fine," she tells him. "I've never had the chance to eat here, but I've heard the entire menu is delicious."

"*Amore,*" he warns. "What is your favorite dish?"

Another nibble. Then she gives in to Dean's overbearingness. "Mushroom risotto."

"Done," he says, snatching up the menus and turning toward the swinging door that leads to the kitchen.

"I—" I begin.

He doesn't acknowledge me, and he sure as shit doesn't take my order. He just tells Marie, "Wine will be out soon," and then disappears into the kitchen, the door swinging closed behind him.

Marie's gaze stays on that swaying metal panel for a long moment.

Then she turns back to me and whispers, "I didn't think that risotto was on the menu."

"It's not," I tell her. "As far as I know—"

But I barely get the words out before a waiter is bustling back in, a bottle of wine in hand. He pours generously then disappears just as quickly, not giving me a chance to order *my* food—and it's not going to be mushroom risotto.

For one, I can't stand risotto.

For another, mushrooms only make the already cloying dish more disgusting.

Which is a thought that's going to remain inside my head.

I don't want my Dean's privileges revoked...or another dozen favors tacked onto my list.

Plus, I need to behave.

Because I have the feeling that not even Molly's peanut butter chocolate chip cookies are going to compare with what Dean whips up.

TWENTY-SEVEN

Marie

FULL BODIED red wine that competes with the best of the best from Jean-Michel's winery.

Crusty sourdough with salted, herbed butter.

A spring salad with a tart dressing, cranberries, walnuts, and goat cheese.

King crab legs and roasted asparagus.

And then—

"Mmm," I moan, eyes closing, tastebuds humming. The mushrooms are divine, earthy with just the perfect amount of chew, the rice is creamy but not mushy, and the slivers of steak positioned throughout the dish are so tender they literally melt in my mouth.

I don't think I've ever had a better bite of food.

Seriously.

And I'm not—or I wasn't—even that hungry when the plate came out, too enamored by the previous dishes to pace myself.

I'm not going to be able to eat daintily now either.

Because it's just too good.

"Now that's the face of a satisfied woman."

My eyes fly open at the husky statement and then just as quickly, I narrow them at the man who caused all this trouble in the first place. It's going to be a miracle if I fit into any of my clothing after tonight. "If I bust the zipper on this dress, it's going to be your fault."

His mouth kicks up and I notice he hasn't started in on his steak—no risotto, just a hearty helping of mashed potatoes on the side. "If you bust your zipper on that dress I'll be very happy."

I snort.

He winks and picks up his fork and knife, cutting off a piece of steak and popping it into his mouth, the soft hum of his pleasure as he chews stroking me right between the thighs.

We've talked about the weather, about my TV show, about the Eagles—and the possibility of him bribing me with more of Molly's confections in order to get free tickets to a playoff game. But we've been interrupted frequently too—by the wine and then the bread, by the salads and refills of our wine, then by the second and more wine. It's not too much, the service polite and controlled (aside from Dean making a couple of appearances to gauge my reaction on the food), but it's meant that we've haven't really gotten going, conversation wise.

His teasing has mostly been kept under wraps by the staff.

And my snark has been tempered by bites of food as we chow down. And Dean.

Case in point?

His head pops through the swinging doors. "How's that risotto, *amore*?"

Jace sighs, but I don't look at him, just smile at Dean. "It's the best dish I've ever eaten—hands down."

"Oh, you flatter me," he prevaricates, though I don't miss the way he preens like a peacock showing off his tail feathers.

"It's not flattery." I smile at him. "It's delicious. Thank you," I add softly. "For taking such good care of us."

"I take care of your stomachs. You let *him*"—a nod at Jace and my eyes flick toward him, see that he's glowering at Dean—"take care of the rest of it."

Jace's face smooths out, and I open my mouth, ready to tell Dean that I can take care of myself, thank you very much, but I don't get the chance to. Because by the time I look back toward the kitchen, he's gone, the door swinging behind him.

"Saved by the escape," Jace says dryly.

Humor slides through my belly. "He's a sweet man."

"He's smitten."

"You sound jealous."

He doesn't reply at first, just saws off another bite of steak, and shoves it into his mouth. So, I go back to my risotto. "You're nice to him."

It's a grudging statement, as though he's surprised he said it at all.

And I still, fork suspended with a hunk of mushroom on the tines. "Excuse me?"

He scowls, and I fucking hate that it's cute, but even as I'm processing that, I'm processing something else, something that sands down the rough edges of my emotions, the ones that have gone spiky and hard ever since I first entered this man's presence.

Though, not that first night on the couch, when he looked tired and young.

They were soft then—open and welcoming.

Same as they were when he was serving up ramen, when he was bringing me cookies, rolling down the bag so they remained fresh.

And...right now.

As I realize what I missed.

He cares. *This* night matters. He all but dragged me into agreeing to this date, has been a pesky presence down the hall from me, but...

He cares what I think.

And he put effort into tonight.

And...Dean *has* been flirting shamelessly, and aside from a few scowls, a couple of grunts, and one narrow-eyed glare when Dean lingered over my hand, he's been letting me have this.

Letting me enjoy my food without judgment. Complimenting my dress. Asking about the things I like. Paying attention and...circling back to bringing me cookies.

Maybe this doesn't have to be like all the other times.

Maybe he's truly not like the other men.

Worry knots my insides for a moment, but I find it doesn't last longer than that. Because my mind is shifting away from all the ways this is certainly going to go bad for me to...

What about what he likes?

And what does his work entail on a daily basis?

And besides hockey, what does *he* like to watch on TV?

And does he read? Definitely not spicy romance novels like me, considering the surprised and indulgent expression on his face in the gym.

And...

I realize I have a hundred questions. No, *more*.

But before I can ask any of them, he leans forward and nudges my plate a centimeter in my direction. "Eat your food, cookie."

"And I'm not nice to you," I murmur, my fork still suspended, those questions now mingling with the tiniest bit of guilt.

I don't owe it to any man to be nice to them.

But...I also know that all of my prickliness isn't because of Jace.

It's because I'm scared.

And curious. And needy. And, despite my best efforts, I like him.

"I earned it, gorgeous," he says. "There's something about you that brings out the wicked in me."

"Jace—"

He cuts off another piece of meat. "It's my fault. Seriously. When you get fired up, your eyes spark and your cheeks go slightly pink, and all I can think about is getting between your legs again."

Plink.

My fork hits my plate and I narrow my eyes at him, annoyance slicing through my middle. "Stop turning me on."

"It's the only time you seem to like me"—he smiles to soften the words—"so...no."

Outrage bubbles up and my cheeks go hot.

Damn. The pesky man is right.

Something I know that he's recognized that *I* know because he winks again, that smile growing. "Eat, cookie."

I want to resist, purely on principle.

But the risotto is too good to waste.

"I'll eat"—triumph in those gorgeous hazel eyes, but I know that my next words will make it short-lived—

Take that, Jace Henderson.

"—but only if you tell me about your deepest darkest secret as I do."

TWENTY-EIGHT

Jace

I NEARLY CHOKE on the bite of steak I just shoved in my mouth.

"What?" I rasp.

She looks so damned proud of herself as she daintily eats her risotto. "You heard me."

"Why do you think I have secrets?"

"Men like you always do."

I frown, take a glug of my wine—which is good enough that, for a moment, I don't want to throttle Dean. Then I focus on the troublesome woman sitting across from me. "Men like me?"

"Rich. Powerful. Determined to get what they want."

She's not wrong on those fronts.

"Determined to get what I want doesn't always mean that I *do* get what I want," I hedge.

"Does it?" she asks archly, scooping up some rice. "Does it really?"

I laugh softly. "Yes, cookie. It means that sometimes I don't get what I want—especially when it's waking up next to a certain gorgeous brunette."

"Even when you could have *any* gorgeous brunette you want?"

"Not true." I nod at her fork when it continues to hover, and she's not eating her food. "And there's a *particular* brunette that I'm in to."

"Because she's a challenge?"

I nod again and this time it makes it into her mouth, and she chews and swallows as I say, "Because she's smart and funny and a hard worker. Because she's clearly been hurt before and that's left her gushy, but she's still out in the world, living her life—"

Something crosses her face but she doesn't speak, just takes another bite of food.

So, I go on, "Because she reads smutty books and watches trashy TV shows but is incredibly good at her job because Jean-Michel doesn't work with people who aren't, *especially* if they don't like hockey."

She grins. "It's not that I don't like hockey."

"No?"

"It's that there are so many better things to watch." One slender, bared shoulder lifts and drops. "Unless there are really good snacks."

I chuckle. "You get me those playoff tickets and I'll definitely up my snack game."

A giggle that makes me feel a hundred feet tall. "You're on."

"You know that means you just agreed to a second date."

"I *know* you didn't answer my question."

"About my deepest darkest secret?"

She taps her nose. "Got it in one."

I cut off another piece of meat, but I don't eat it, not yet, not when there's part of me that wants to share. Because she's asking. Because she wants to know the answer. Because it might mean that she'll share some of the same with me. "I don't know if I'd call it my deepest darkest secret—I'm pretty much an open book—"

She snorts.

"No?"

"Come on," she says. "You're...*you*. The elusive Jace Henderson, billionaire by the time you were twenty-nine, perpetual bachelor who takes on health insurance companies and government officials alike."

"That's probably why my patent application was denied," I mutter.

She frowns. "For the blood clot removal product you're testing?"

"You know about that?"

Titan Capital and Genen-core collaborate in the loosest of terms—Titan Capital provides the silent capital for the producer of one of the microchips in our product—but that's not under Marie's purview.

Or maybe...I misjudged how much she actually does.

Or maybe not, I realize when I see the edgy look creep onto her face. "What?" I ask.

Surprisingly, she answers, "I may or may not have done some research on you when I found out you lived down the hall."

"She likes me, folks," I tease. "I think she really likes me."

She keeps going. "And anyway, so I read up on Genen-core." A shrug. "What you're doing is pretty cool." One half of her mouth tips up. "And it's even cooler that Titan Capital can claim a small part of it."

"More of your research?"

"I'm good at my job." Her nose wrinkles. "Though, I suppose I can't reasonably take credit for saving tens of thousands of lives now, can I?"

I grin. "Maybe not."

"Drat." She scoops up the last bite of her risotto. "So, why did the patent get denied?"

"So far our legal team doesn't have any concrete answers. They say our item isn't patentable, but that's bullshit and we have the research and precedence to prove it." I sigh, a familiar throb beginning in my temple. I've been going over and over this in my head, without making much progress. "And bullshit seems to be a problem that's catching all around—there's weird shit happening, some of it feels punitive in nature, and no matter how hard we try, no real answers are unearthed and we can't get ahead of it."

"Hmm," she says quietly.

I push my plate back, suddenly not able to stomach the last few bites, no matter how delicious. "I've had to put out more than a fair share of fires in regard to contract renewals and distribution agreements, and that's not even taking into account the patent, or the fact that the board's not happy, or...that I'm getting the sinking sensation that someone in my organization is actively trying to sabotage the company."

Her brows pull together. "Do you have any leads?"

"Unfortunately not." I sigh, finish off my wine because at least the red will hone down the sharp edges of my frustration. "Worse, we seem to be involved in a certain powerful bureau's investigation, though I don't have any fucking answers on that front either."

"Does that bureau go by a name that's only three letters long?"

I put my wine glass down. "Yes," I say slowly.

She picks hers up, takes a long sip. "I know this is unlikely, considering the minuscule connection between our companies, but my intuition is screaming at me."

"What's it saying?"

"That it's too early to put my cards on the table, but that I promise to do some research tomorrow and let you know as soon as I have something concrete."

I study her for a long moment.

Then I figure she's fully capable of handling this, and that if she does find something pertaining to Genen-core, she'll share it.

So I just say, "Okay."

Her eyes go wide. "Just...*okay?*"

"Yeah, cookie. Just okay. Let me know if there's anything I can do to help, but otherwise...I've spent a while trying to figure this shit out on my own. If someone as smart as you wants to take a crack at it, I'm down."

Her mouth opens.

Closes.

Then opens again.

But before she can reply to me, the door to the kitchen swings open and Dean is reappearing, a waiter on his heels.

They sweep away the dredges of our entrees, deposit coffees and decadent desserts in front of us.

And then Marie is smiling up at me, scooping her spoon into the chocolate mousse, and she asks, "What kind of books do you read?"

We spend the rest of our time at Dean's discussing books that we've read and places we've traveled to and the locations that are still on our bucket lists.

There isn't any tension.

But there is plenty of laughter and teasing, and when I

leave her just inside her front door, after having kissed her long enough for my control to begin to unravel, she doesn't press me for one more night—and *only* one night.

Instead, she smiles as I step back out into the hall, and says...

"Don't think I forgot about the deepest, darkest secret part."

TWENTY-NINE

Marie

I'M bleary-eyed and knee deep—or maybe elbow deep—in papers when I find it...with more than a little help from an employee named Suzanne.

She was caught in Angela's web of deceit a few weeks back, reached out to Jean-Michel.

And...another thread.

Another person not willing to let all these strange coincidences go.

Today, it's her email that sets me down a path I hadn't thoroughly inspected before.

And it gives me a connection between Titan Capital and Genen-core...and it's not solely that tiny microchip distributer.

It's...more.

Immediately, I reach for my phone, wanting to call Jace.

But I freeze a heartbeat after I unlock the screen.

Because I don't have the man's number.

God, why am I such a stubborn pain in the ass?

Scowling, I toss my phone on my desk and pack up the files, shoving them into my bag, emailing myself copies of documents from my work computer I won't have access to at home, grabbing anything that I might need to finish puzzling this shit out.

Then I slip out of the empty office, everyone having gone home hours ago.

Down the elevator, to my car, out of the lot.

I stop in the driveway, waiting for the signal, but as I turn in the direction of my building, there's a flash of light out of the corner of my eye.

Bright enough that the turn in the evening's dusk becomes difficult and I have to swerve around a female pedestrian crossing outside the crosswalk.

Not unusual—sometimes those white zebra lines are just a suggestion.

But paired with the flash of light and...

I take a second look.

The woman is tall and blond and slender, wearing dark clothes and sunglasses, even though the sun has set. And she looks familiar.

She looks like Angela Rosseau, Jean-Michel's ex-wife.

A horn beeps behind me and I realize that I've stopped in the middle of the road.

I look back at the woman.

But she's gone.

"What the fuck?" I whisper before pushing on the accelerator so the guy behind me doesn't have a conniption.

Then I drive home—with no further flashes of light or strange women in dark clothes and sunglasses or horns being blared at me.

I pull into my spot, hurry over to the elevators, impatiently waiting as it brings me up to my floor.

It seems to take forever—and I don't know if it's because of what I found or because I'm looking forward to seeing Jace.

I worry it may be the latter.

But, after last night, maybe not as much as I should.

The doors open with a ding, and I step off, not even stopping at my place, just going straight down the hall and around the corner to Jace's condo.

My heart starts pounding as I lift a hand, start to knock.

Then stop.

Because even though I can all but hear Jace's annoying as hell *bawk-bawking* in my head, I'm a chicken shit.

This is me going to him.

This isn't me waiting at home, speculating whether or not (or maybe hoping) that he'll show up, demanding to be let in.

This is...another step toward potential heartbreak.

"Or it's finally solving this shit with Angela, you drama queen," I mutter, "and helping out two companies under attack in the process." A beat as I shore up my spine. "So, quit dicking around and knock on the fucking door."

Suitably chastised, I lift my hand again, ball my fingers into a fist, and I knock.

Is it barely audible and completely pathetic? Yes.

But do I hold my ground and not retreat back down the hall to the safety of my woman cave? Also, yes.

Unfortunately, even though I count to ninety, Jace doesn't answer.

So, I'm forced to knock again.

And this time to do it with more authority.

It echoes through the hall and I pair it with the doorbell a few minutes later (see? I was totally being a chicken shit).

But both of those go unanswered.

And then I'm left, still in the damn hallway, urgency

nibbling at my bones, and second-guessing the shit out of myself.

I nibble my bottom lip, knock one more time, and hang in the hall for a couple of moments longer.

Maybe he's in the shower.

Maybe he's traveling for work. No. He would have said something last night. I'm sure of it.

But...work!

Maybe he's still at work. As in, maybe he's still at his office. I was working late, catching up on everything, so maybe he's doing the same.

I start back down the hall, disappointment curling through my middle.

I'll wait for him, listen for the elevators, or come back later and knock again...

My heart squeezes.

Because I don't *want* to wait.

Because that pesky itch to see him is tickling my nape, the space between my shoulder blades.

"Dumb," I whisper.

Still, when I reach my door, I pause, but I don't get my keys out, don't unlock the door, don't go inside. Instead...I keep walking, not stopping until I'm by the elevators, until I'm pushing the button for the garage level.

Off I go again, the internal *bawk-bawking* loud enough that my footsteps don't falter as I stride back over to my car, as I get inside and hook up my phone, the navigation guiding me to Genen-core's corporate offices.

I have no idea how I'll find Jace once I'm there...

But I'm resourceful.

And I'm not thinking about all the ways this might blow up in my face.

"There. Good," I mutter, pulling out of my building

without having to navigate flashing lights or horns or sunglass-wearing women.

The drive takes less than ten minutes during this time of night—something I'm grateful for, considering that Marie Chicken Shit is raring her ugly head, reminding me of all the times I put myself out there...and all the times doing so backfired.

So much so that by the time I reach the campus and pause next to the guard station, my heart is pounding in my chest as I scramble to come up with some reason why I'm here after business hours without permission, and definitely without a guest pass.

But the little guard shack is empty and the arm is raised, and so I just...drive through.

I point my car in the direction of the tallest building, both because it's the tallest, and also because it's the only one with lights on inside and cars in the adjacent lot.

"I'll find security," I whisper, psyching myself up. "Ask them to call him."

Simple. Easy. Done.

So why does it feel as though I'm standing in the open doorway of a plane, a parachute strapped to my back, being told to jump.

Because...

I'm putting myself out there.

"Ugh," I mutter, snagging my bag and shoving open my door.

I walk up to the building, am surprised when the glass door opens when I tug it—no keycard required, no security manning the front desk to greet me or buzz me in.

I move inside, and it's empty.

Not a person in sight to stop me from moving to the elevators, from glancing at the directory on the wall.

From finding out exactly what floor Jace's office is on.

What. The. Fuck?

Anger begins boiling through me and I jab at the button, climb onto the car, then jab at the next button, the one that will take me up to his floor.

And still no one stops me.

Does the man have no sense of self-preservation?

I growl when the doors close, huff out an annoyed breath when they open again, eight floors up, showing me a darkened floor...

Except for one corner office.

And that's when my temper snaps.

THIRTY

Jace

"TELL me you didn't fuck things up last night."

I close out of my windows, shut down my computer, and lean back in my chair. "You've been here two minutes," I mutter. "And you're already giving me shit?"

"You told me you think you've met the woman you want to make yours—"

I ignore the blip of worry in my stomach, the one that reminds me that I want her, that I like her a fucking lot, but that I still might do something to fuck it up. That I might hurt her and not be able to fix it and—

"And you're sitting in your office, working late, twiddling your thumbs instead of going to her."

"I had to practically bully her into a first date...and then barge into her apartment to make sure she actually came."

Brooks grins.

I glare at him. "She was sweet as pie to Dean, ate with an abandon that made me want to get her right back into the bedroom, and actually opened up to me a little," I say, or maybe remind him since I already gave the nosy fuck the full report last night after I got home from Marie's place. "I made progress, man. I need to move deliberately now, so I don't fuck it up."

"Or you need to actually *move* instead of letting her erect walls around herself again that you need to bust through."

I scowl.

Because he's not wrong.

And because when Brooks isn't wrong, he's a smug pain in the ass.

"When are you going back to France?" I ask. It's my most common rejoinder with him of late.

He grins, not missing the surly note in my voice. "Nah, man. I think I'm going to move here permanently. I actually put in an offer on a house near Oak Ridge."

Christ.

"The office building or the winery?" I ask, head pounding at the thought of him living on the next floor down or somewhere equally as close.

"The winery."

Thank fuck for small miracles.

But still too near to stick his nosy ass into my business.

"Maybe you'll find a sexy neighbor to keep you busy," I say, going for distraction.

"Nah," he mutters. "A woman isn't on the docket for me."

"A man then?"

His head jerks and he grins at me. "You're a child."

"A child," I say, reaching for my phone and shoving it into my pocket, "who's going to get the fuck out of here and take your advice about going and getting my woman."

He grins, stands up. "Damn right you are. And keep me on speed dial if you need any further advice."

"You mean if you want to demand any further details?"

"Both things can be right."

I snort, push to my feet, but before I can snipe back, there's a knock. I look...just in time to see the door push inward.

A flash of curls.

A gorgeous woman.

Who's scowling at me.

"Your security sucks," she snaps, pushing fully inside. "Do you know that I was just able to park, access this building—which has a directory listing your fucking floor!—and take the elevator, walk over, and enter your office without a single person stopping me." She tosses up her hands. "You're the CEO of a multi-billion-dollar business with the personal net worth that's more than most people can even dream about amassing in their lifetimes! Do you even care about your safety? What if some psycho got a wild hair and decided to come up here and—"

Brooks chuckles.

And I have to force down my own amusement when I watch her face change as she realizes we're not alone.

Pink cheeks. Horror traipsing through her expression. She closes her eyes for a heartbeat. Two. Then her chin comes up and her shoulders straighten.

She extends her hand toward Brooks. "Marie."

"Brooks," he says, lips twitching, tone amused. "Nice to meet you."

"I—uh—nice to meet you too."

Silence falls, and I glare at my friend. Mostly because he's still holding Marie's hand.

And she doesn't seem to be bothered by the contact.

"How do you know Jace?" he asks, even though he knows perfectly well, the bastard.

"We, um..." Bright pink cheeks and she finally tugs her hand back, eyes darting to the door, clearly looking for the exit.

"Obviously, you guys are in the middle of something. I should"
—she hitches a thumb over her shoulder—"go."

My body jerks forward, every cell screaming *absolutely fucking not*.

But Brooks beats me to doing or saying anything stupid. "I was actually just heading out." He touches her shoulder, hovering close enough that I want to murder him for intruding on *my* woman's space. Then again when he says, "It was nice to put a name to a face. He talks about you all the time."

Wide green eyes hit mine.

"And," the fucker goes on, "don't stop giving him crap about the security. I've mentioned that shit to him at least a half dozen times and there's no change."

Murder. Times three.

I swear to fuck.

But I don't get the chance to throttle my best friend because he's slipping out of the room without a backward glance at me.

Leaving me with a now *un*embarrassed Marie.

In fact, she's so far from embarrassed it's not funny.

Because she's *pissed*.

At me.

As soon as the door closes, she marches over to me, dropping her bag in the chair Brooks recently vacated, stomping around the corner of my desk, not stopping until her toes brush mine. She jabs a finger into my chest.

"Ow," I mutter, capturing her hand in mine and then rubbing the aching spot with my other.

Her eyes spark with fury. "You're telling me that someone has brought the lackluster security to your attention and you haven't done anything about it?"

I open my mouth to explain.

But I don't get the chance.

"You're a well-known, important man who's doing important work. Do you truly not give a fuck about your safety?" A shake of her head as she tries to tug her hand free, but she's close and smells like flowers and her body is pressed to mine and...she's *here.* So I'm not fucking letting her go. Something she seems to realize a moment later when she continues snapping, "And if you're so arrogant to not care about being safe, do you not understand that it can impact the safety of your employees? You're doing important work here and they need to feel secure to make the most of it."

"I know."

"You have an unmanned security shed at the entrance of your campus, an unmanned security desk downstairs, unlocked doors, elevators than can be accessed by anyone—"

"I know, cookie."

"It's so dangerous!" she exclaims. "I don't know why you can't—"

I cup her jaw. "I *know,* cookie," I repeat, finally managing to cut off the flow of words. "Security's been a problem ever since we contracted with a new company. I'm working on it, especially because there's absolutely no reason the doors downstairs should have been unlocked. We have a badge system for a reason and pay for twenty-four hour guards, but Duarte—"

She jerks in my hold, so violently that I lose my grip on her.

And then she's turning away from me.

Stepping back.

And running away.

THIRTY-ONE

Marie

OH, my God.

I'm an idiot.

Literally an idiot.

I came here to share information with him, to get on the same page—okay, no. I came because it's important for him to know this, but it didn't—or maybe it *shouldn't*—have come before me telling Attie.

And then, instead of after relaying my information to Agent Phillips, calmly telling Jace about what I discovered, I throw a fit. In front of Brooks freaking Saxton no less.

Another billionaire.

This of the quieter variety.

He's not in the press much, and he lives out of the country, but I know he controls an important investment fund that has had its hands in many a Bay Area tech start up.

He's also in crypto.

And...I'm losing my mind.

Having a temper tantrum in front of him, yelling at Jace like a psycho, and worst of all, doing it so intensely that I fucking forgot why I was here.

Dumb.

Dumb.

"Cookie—" Jace begins as I shove away from him and start sprinting toward my bag.

I want to snatch it up and run out of here, but I know this is more important than my crippling embarrassment.

"Freeze right there."

The tone is one I haven't heard from him before.

Hell, I don't think I've heard it from anyone, not even Jean-Michel when he's at his bossiest.

And it doesn't do what I would expect—doesn't raise my hackles and have me snapping at him again.

Instead...I freeze, phantom fingers stroking me between my thighs, heat blooming in my middle.

And he seems to recognize it too.

"You like that."

"No." My throat works, and I will my feet to carry me forward, but I can't make them move, not as I hear his footsteps as he prowls toward me.

He shifts my hair, sliding it over the opposite shoulder, lips coming to my ear. "You do."

"I—"

His hand settles on my waist, drawing me back against him.

"Should we talk about why you came?" he asks silkily, mouth drifting along my jaw, tracing lightly enough to make me shiver against him.

"I—"

"Or should we discuss why you're turned on when I gave you an order? Or maybe"—his lips press to my throat—"I should order you to get naked and place your hands flat on the desk."

Heat scorches me from the inside, and I know he feels it when I tremble, when my knees threaten to give way, when my hips arch back against him, ass rubbing against the hardening length of his erection. "We sh-should talk about why I came."

"Hmm." A flash of teeth. "Okay then, gorgeous. Tell me why you're here."

"I figured it out."

His hand has been trailing up and down my side, and it doesn't stop. "The connection between Titan Capital and Genen-core?"

"Mmm—*ah!*" I gasp when his fingertips brush the bottom of my breast.

"What's that, cookie?"

"Yes," I manage to push out. "I found the connection."

"And is that connection going to change in the next thirty —" A beat as his palm slides down, cupping my hip, drawing me more firmly against him. "Scratch that. The next forty-five minutes?"

Forty-five minutes of this man touching me, holding me, kissing and stroking and fu—

"No," I rasp. "It's not going to change."

A rough chuckle. "Good."

He steps back, and I wobble slightly.

He steadies me but doesn't come close again, doesn't kiss my skin or stroke his hands over me or hold me close.

Instead, he moves to the door and locks it.

Then to the wide plate glass windows and closes the blinds.

"Marie," he says and that firm tone has my head jerking up, has desire gathering between my thighs. "Take off your..."

My heart skips a beat.

My knees tremble again.

"...shoes, cookie."

A curl of disappointment. But also a thrill of excitement.

Because am I doing this? Is this happening? Is—

"*Gorgeous.*"

My eyes fly back to his.

"Shoes."

Pulse skittering through my veins, I step out of my shoes, kicking them to the side. But when I reach for the lapels of my jacket, he tuts.

"I didn't tell you to take that off yet."

I freeze, another thrill sliding through me. I like it—these orders—and probably more than I should. But I'm also still me. So, even though I don't tear off my jacket out of spite, I still say, "Kind of hard for me to get naked and bend over the desk if you won't let me take off my clothes, handsome."

His mouth curves, and the sexy smile has that desire between my legs growing.

Especially as he saunters toward me. "Smart," he murmurs, trailing a finger along the row of buttons on my blouse. Down, down, *down* it goes.

And so does he, kneeling in front of me, reaching for my foot, and—

I moan as his strong fingers begin massaging, soothing the aching toes, the sore arch, the tight ankle in long, sure strokes. He doesn't say anything and I'm not capable of a response as he pays homage to my feet over the next several minutes, first one and then the other, thoroughly reducing me to goo.

Then he pauses, one of my feet on his broad, strong thigh, and looks up at me. "Take off your jacket, gorgeous."

My throat works.

Then I oblige, lifting my hands to the edges of my blazer, dragging it down my arms.

He catches it before it puddles to the floor, draping it carefully over the chair.

"Is this when I get naked?" I ask.

He grins before he lifts my foot to his mouth, pressing a kiss to the top of it. Then he's setting it on the floor, slowly standing.

He stands close but doesn't touch me.

Hot hazel eyes on mine. They slowly drift down my body, and that stare is almost a physical thing, stroking over my nipples, down my abdomen, dipping between my legs.

"Take your shirt off," he orders quietly

I almost jump to comply with the order, hands jerking up toward my buttons—

"Slow down, cookie."

I listen, fingers shaking slightly as I undo the fastenings, incrementally revealing my naked flesh. It's harder to keep my movements steady when despite the calm voice, the steady expression, I don't miss his eyes going even hotter and his hands clenching into tighter and tighter fists with each inch of my skin that's exposed.

He wants to touch.

But he also knows I'm getting off on this—well, he is too, considering the erection tenting his pants.

Still, it's more than desire I'm feeling, at least for a moment.

Because he's trying something that I like, for no other reason than...I like it.

And I know there's no going back.

I'm falling for this man.

"Stop there," he orders, his voice more rasp than anything when I reach the last button.

"Still not naked," I breathe.

A twitch of his lips. "Undo the button on your pants."

I flick it open.

"The zipper too."

The *ziiip* is loud in the quiet office.

"Push the fabric down."

I nudge at the loose material at my waist and my pants drop to the floor. I inhale in a rush when the cold hits my bare skin, but it's his groan that really captures my attention.

"Fuck, gorgeous," he growls. "You wear *that* under those prim and proper clothes?"

My gaze drifts down to the black lace, and I'm about to confess that I put it on because I was thinking about him this morning.

But he orders, "Shirt off," and I hurry to comply.

He doesn't gather my pants or my blouse, just leaves them in crumpled piles on the floor as he steps closer, those eyes taking in every inch of me. "Fuck me," he growls. "You are so damned beautiful."

My heart leaps.

And then my pussy spasms.

Because he orders, "Turn around and put your hands flat on the desk."

THIRTY-TWO

Jace

MY CONTROL IS SHREDDED.

She's so fucking beautiful.

And she came to my office.

And she worried about me.

And she's wearing the sexiest set of underwear I have ever seen—black lace and so fucking skimpy it barely covers anything.

Through that sheer fabric, I can see the rosy buds of her nipples, the plump pink lips of her pussy.

And in between...it's nothing but miles and miles of naked skin.

Her mouth parts on an exhale, the pink growing on her cheeks, spreading down along her chest.

But then she slowly turns around, giving me a glimpse of the back of her G-string.

I curse, take a step toward her, wanting to rip that tiny scrap of fabric off, to spread her legs, and plunge deep inside.

Patience.

I haven't even touched her yet.

I need to make this good for her.

Because it's fucking great for me right about now.

I trail a finger around the tiny strip of elastic that makes up the back of her panties, following it over the curve of one cheek and then the other.

"I imagined you doing this when I put them on this morning."

I keep tracing, dipping down into the cleft.

She gasps softly, spreads her legs, and I take the silent message, moving down and in, sliding my fingers through her slick pussy.

"Jace," she moans.

A flick to her clit, and then I'm slipping my hand free, undoing the clasp of her bra, cupping both of her breasts, massaging the soft globes, rolling the buds of her nipples, watching that ass bounce as her hips buck and she tries to seek purchase against me.

Something I don't allow, not quite yet.

Because if I do, this will all be over far too fast.

So, I work her breasts and I watch her ass, and eventually I kiss my way down her spine, kneeling behind her, drawing her underwear down her legs.

"Jace," she whispers, starting to turn.

"Hands on that desk, gorgeous."

A jerk, her hips bucking.

"Good," I croon. "Now spread your legs."

Her inhale is sharp, my name tumbling off her lips again.

And then those legs inch apart.

I'm the one saying her name now. I lean closer, drag a finger through that slick heat.

"Such a pretty pussy," I croon. "Do you want me to lick it?"

"*Jace.*" She shifts back, inching closer to my face, silently telling me she wants my mouth there.

"Mmm." I dip another finger in, circle her entrance. "Why don't you ask me nicely to lick this slick cunt of yours, gorgeous? And then I'll decide whether or not you've been good enough for you to come on my tongue."

Another tremble. Another "*Jace.*"

But I don't give us what we both want.

Not until she spreads her legs an inch further and then asks, "Will you lick my pussy until I come, handsome?"

"Hmm." Another slow trail of my finger.

But I'm already leaning in.

And I'm tasting her—the soft, floral musk of her, the slick, slick evidence of her desire. I slide my tongue inside, feel the walls of her cunt already spasming, and reach my hand forward, rolling my thumb over her clit, pressing firmly enough for her to cry out and jerk against me. I don't stop, just help her ride the edge of the pleasure, driving her higher, knowing it's not going to be long before I get to hear her fall apart, get to be inside her, get to—

"Jace!"

She grinds her pussy back against my face, rides my fingers and my tongue.

Her moan is long and drawn out, her gorgeous body slumping as she lays flat on my desk, that plump ass in the air.

I slowly leave her, trailing my hands over her body, just watching her.

So fucking beautiful.

And mine.

Something I know with absolute certainty when she slowly lifts her head, glancing at me over her shoulder. "Is it time for me to give an order now?" she asks lazily.

I grin, even though my dick is so hard it could pound nails. "Depends on what that order is, cookie."

Her eyes fill with mischief.

And heat.

"Fuck me, Jace. Hard and fast and—"

I'm moving before I realize, shoving my pants down, stepping between her legs, thrusting home and—

I groan.

She hisses out a breath.

"Too much?"

"No, handsome," she says softly. "Just right." She arches against me, taking me deeper, and...

It's over then.

My attempts at control, at going slow, at making this last even longer.

I fuck her, the aforementioned hard and fast, adding in deep and rough and not stopping as my orgasm flies toward me. Because she's there too, hot and slick, moaning my name, thrusting back against me, as mindless in seeking pleasure as I am.

Then it's on me, and thankfully, she's right there with me, coming apart moments after me, drawing out my pleasure until I'm barely standing.

And then I'm not on my feet any longer.

I'm slowly collapsing to the floor, thankfully with enough presence of mind to gather her against me and cradle her close as we make our descent.

It's not until our breaths slow and my head stops spinning before she speaks again.

"Next time I get to give the orders."

And even though I had an orgasm that all but split me in half, I find that I'm laughing.

THIRTY-THREE

Marie

IT TOOK us a long time to summon the energy to get dressed.

And even longer before I managed to focus enough to grab my bag and pull out the files.

We sit, side by side, and I tap at the one in front of him.

"When were you going to tell me that you owned the building we both live in?"

He glances at me then right back at the page I printed out.

But I don't miss his sheepish smile.

I certainly hear the chagrin in his words, though, when he says, "It didn't matter."

My eyebrows flick up. "And all those times you conveniently ran into me were just coincidence?" I ask dryly.

He pulls the folder closer, as though he's studiously absorbing every word.

I clear my throat. "Well?"

"Well what?"

How can a man who brought me so much pleasure, also

drive me so insane? "Were those times you ran into me coincidences?"

"If I say yes, will you believe me?"

"No." I roll my eyes, but I'm smiling, and I don't fight him when he disturbs the papers by pulling me into his lap. It feels so good that I let him, ignoring his huff of laughter, and settling on his chest.

"I was determined not to like you, you know," I murmur long moments later.

"Yup." I still in surprise. "Hence needing those coincidences."

I giggle. "You're incorrigible."

"You've called me worse things and I've liked those too."

I giggle again, but before I can go back to the papers I brought, he asks, "How'd you find out about the building, anyway?"

"About you owning it?"

He smooths back my hair. "Yeah, gorgeous," he says. "It's in a trust and usually that creates enough distance between my properties and myself."

A flicker of pride sliding through me. "I'm good at what I do."

"Yeah, you are." He kisses the top of my head. "I'll have to tell my lawyers to be trickier to keep you on your toes."

"That won't stop me, muahaha."

He chuckles, draws me closer. "I'm sure it won't."

I want to just hang here, cuddled against him, and not think about Angela or the FBI or corporate sabotage. But this is important, and he needs to know.

"I found the trust because the same realtor who sold Angela a house, also sold properties to your trust, Duarte Enterprises, and one of your head scientists on the blood clot research project."

I feel his body tense. "What?"

"I have his name here." I pass him the file.

"Dammit," he curses softly as he reads through the papers. "I really liked him."

"I don't know for sure if he's sabotaging anything or involved with the issues with your patent, but it's suspect."

"It is," he agrees.

"I'll give FBI the information, make sure they loop you in on next steps because acting too quickly on this might tip him off and spook him."

"You're right," he says. "And Duarte?"

"Duarte is a security company. They have government contracts, and one of their subsidiaries runs private security for—"

"Companies like mine," he murmurs. "That's why you went still before when I mentioned their name."

"Yes."

He sighs. "Their services are a nightmare, though. They've been nothing but trouble from the moment we signed the contract. You got a taste of that tonight with the unlocked doors and unmanned desks."

A flicker of worry slides through me. "They're not providing the contracted services."

"No," he agrees. "Or not to the capacity they should be doing. Legal is working on getting us out of the contract, but they're shifty, and though we're working on bringing in a new company in the meantime, this shit has gotten very complicated with about a hundred hoops to jump through."

"I know."

His brows shoot up. "You know?"

"They do security for Titan Capital too," I tell him, snagging a paper and passing it over to him. "And we've had some of the same problems—or *had* before Jean-Michel chewed out the owner, made suitable threats, and they finally got their shit together."

"I guess I need to work on my scary face."

I chuckle even though nothing about this is amusing. "Maybe. He's also brought in another firm to backfill and keep an eye on the Duarte guys."

"That's a good idea."

"It's still a tangle," I say, barely resisting the urge to scrub my hands over my face. "And expensive. But between the real estate connections and the security contracts I think this is big enough of a connection to pass on to my contact at the FBI."

"Agent Phillips?"

"She gets around, huh?" I say dryly.

"Apparently." His mouth quirks. "I met her the first time the other day—she seems whip smart and fully capable."

"Make sure you call her Attie next time you see her," I slide in, feeling slightly jealous. Whip smart? Capable?

Then I mentally smack myself.

It's not like he's saying she's gorgeous...which, of course, she is.

"She like that?" he asks, eyes twinkling.

"It's her favorite."

He taps me on the tip of my nose. "Always mischief-making." Then he leans close, nuzzles my throat. "Always beautiful."

And I melt.

Especially, when he says, "I knew you'd solve it."

"What?"

"I knew you'd put the pieces together far faster than I could."

"They're not fully together yet and anyway, you would have—"

"No, I wouldn't." A kiss to my jaw. "Now, any other revelations?"

"Not at this moment."

A grin. "Good."

We sit there for a moment, cuddled up and content. Then he smooths my curls back and gently sets me to the side, gathering up the papers and tucking them into my bag. Then he stands and extends a hand.

"Let's get out of here."

A tug brings me to my feet.

"Your place or mine?" I ask.

He smiles, and I know that I'll remember it forever.

Same as his next words sew themselves into my soul.

"It doesn't matter, cookie. Because wherever you are feels like home."

THIRTY-FOUR

Jace

"I'VE BEEN SELFISH," she murmurs, early the next morning.

This is the first morning I've woken up beside her, so I'm just enjoying her body pressed to mine, enjoying the fact that she's here, enjoying that we seem to be moving forward, fucking *finally*.

So her being selfish is pretty much the last thing on my mind.

"I think the fact that I had three orgasms last night is the antithesis of you being selfish, cookie."

She smiles, swatting me lightly on my chest.

Then her expression goes serious.

"I've been so busy putting up walls that I don't really know anything about you." She pushes up on my front, quickly shaking her head. "No, that came out wrong. I know you're kind and thoughtful. I know you're persistent and a hard worker. I know you pay attention and that you have a good friend in Brooks and that you hate risotto."

My lips quirk. "Well clearly, you pay attention too."

Her expression goes soft. "And I know whatever was in the news," she says softly. "I know that you started Genen-core after your mom died of complications from a blood clot and that you're now the leading clot removal product in the world."

"Then you know most of it," I tell her. "My mom died from a pulmonary embolism; the clot broke off and caused a stroke and—" My throat goes tight.

"We don't have to talk about this," she whispers. "I know I sprang it on you and—"

I touch her cheek. "It's okay. She had a lot of health problems, so in a way it was a relief to see she was finally out of pain. It's just...she was a single mom and did her best, but there wasn't a lot of room for me with all of her illnesses, and I was resentful that they took up so much space...and then that, from the moment I was old enough, I was expected to step up and take care of her."

"How old was old enough?" she asks softly.

"Twelve was the first time I called my mom's doctor with a problem."

"So young," she whispers.

"If it wasn't me, no one else would have been able to do it."

"But it *was* you, and you were too young, so I think that some resentment is understandable. I had both parents and they were healthy, but they couldn't be what I needed, and God knows, that messed me up for a long time."

I stroke a finger along silky skin. "What do you mean they couldn't be what you needed?"

"My dad was abusive—physically," she adds matter-of-factly, and I can't stop the rage from encroaching on my vision, from narrowing it to a tiny point that is solely filled by this woman. "He hit my mom. He hit me...until I was old enough to protect myself."

"How could you protect yourself against a grown man?" I rasp.

Her hand finds mine, lacing our fingers together. "I'm okay," she says. "Safe and whole, and he found out that I have a natural inclination for softball."

I appreciate that she's trying to lighten the mood.

I still want to hunt the fucker down and make his life a misery. "You introduced him to your bat?"

A nod. "Luckily, I got my smarts from him, and he was a fast learner. I made it clear that if he kept his distance and stopped hitting my mom that a repeat of the events would never happen...and I'd make sure that it stayed under wraps."

I frown.

"For him, ego was everything."

"Was?"

A nod. "He died about eight years back, six months after my mom. Turns out being a selfish leech your whole life makes it hard to take care of yourself. I was low contact from the time I left for college. It was the only way to survive. Unfortunately, the wounds he left ran deep."

"How, gorgeous?"

"I picked bad men—selfish, mostly. Emotionally manipulative, for sure. And"—she sighs and my rage ramps up because I know her next words are going to infuriate me—"the last one hit me."

I curse. "Please tell me you have his name and address because that fucker is going to *pay*."

"So blood-thirsty," she murmurs, lightly running her hand over my front. "But sadly for you, Jean-Michel found out and he took care of it. Last I heard, Oscar had to move back to Iowa and was living with his parents because he was downsized and couldn't get a job."

"Jean-Michel blacklisted him?"

She nods. "And had a pointed conversation with the owner of the company Oscar worked for. It didn't take long for him to be sent packing." Her hand slides back up, and she cups my jaw. "But this is mostly me talking, handsome, which isn't helping my selfish streak."

"You need to stop talking bad about my woman."

"Trouble."

"Me?"

"Definitely you," she murmurs, pressing her lips to my jaw. "You're far too charming for your own good."

"Or maybe *your* good."

Laughter in the air. "Oh, we know that already, considering how much I fought ending up right here."

I tug at a curl and she leans in, lips brushing over mine. "Will you tell me?"

"Tell you what?"

"That deepest darkest secret," she whispers. "Because I think it's why your eyes go extra sad when you talk about your mom."

"It's hard to lose a parent."

"That's true enough."

"Enough?" I lift my eyebrows in question.

"Yes," she says. "That's true enough, but I don't think it's the reason your grief and regret cling to your words when you speak of her."

She's right.

Of course she is.

But—

"It's not pleasant, cookie."

Her eyes gentle. "It wouldn't be your deepest darkest secret if it was."

She's right again.

Of course she is.

"My mom wasn't abusive, but she took up a lot of emotional energy, and one night just after I graduated college, I wanted to just be a twenty-two-year-old, you know? I wanted to drink with my friends and not think about anything doctor related for one night. No emails to her care team or visits to pharmacies, no phone calls to the insurance company. Just me and my friends and the hot girls who wanted to grind on me in the club."

Marie smiles. "You wanted to be free for a night."

"Yeah," I say. "And I did all the prep work—I got her set up with food and a night nurse, spent time with her that afternoon because she always said I was too busy for her." I feel my throat grow tight again and pause to breathe. Marie doesn't push, just gives me the time to find the next words. "She called, and I stepped outside to answer—she didn't like the nurse, said she was mean. I spent some time mediating that and went back inside." A deep breath. "But she called again, and it was the same shit. So, when she called a third time and a fourth and"—my eyes burn—"a tenth, I didn't pick up the calls. I sent them to voicemail, ordered another drink, and I had my night."

Marie's fingers are wrapped tightly around mine, and she seems to be barely breathing.

I'm doing the same.

Because ripping this out of me is taking all the air in my lungs, all the strength in my body.

"I don't remember the last thing I said to her—I was too drunk. But the words were sharp and impatient and...I didn't fucking pick up the phone."

She slips her hand free from mine, but before I can mourn

the loss of contact, she's wrapping her arms around me and hugging me tight. "I'm so sorry, honey."

"It's my fault. I should have done more, should have been more patient, should—"

"You were a kid." A squeeze of her arms. "You were put in an untenable situation and did the best you could."

I touch her cheek. "So my therapist says." My mouth curves up. "You asked my deepest darkest secret, and that's it, cookie. I have regrets, big ones that seem to swell up and try to take over. But I've made good things happen out of those regrets and we're not stopping with clots. We're putting more research into women's health, because it's chronically underfunded and studies are few and far between. That's the penance I need to pay."

"But—"

"For myself," I tell her. "To soothe those regrets. To fulfill the promise I made when I found her the next morning, already gone. I won't sit in guilt, won't allow it to make me impotent. I'll do something about it, and I'll make the world better for women like her."

"That's beautiful."

"That's the lesson I learned from my mom." I settle my forehead against hers. "When everything else is too heavy, when the fears creep in that I'm not doing enough in my work or I should keep my distance from a certain stubborn brunette before I get too attached and risk ruining what's between us, that's what I can cling to."

"Jace," she whispers.

"And it helps that I have a best friend who kicks my ass when necessary."

"Brooks?"

I nod. "He had to walk away from a relationship, and it cost him almost everything. Not living with the regrets he has meant—*means*—that I know what's between us is worth fighting for."

"Dammit," she whispers.

I push back her hair. "What?"

"You're far too charming for your own good."

"And that's a bad thing?"

"It is when we have to play it cool in front of Jean-Michel. I want to get this stuff straightened out with the FBI and Duarte before I have to run the gauntlet of my interfering, protective boss."

"You know that I know, Jean-Michel, right?"

"Of course you do." A shake of her head, her curls bouncing. "Just not like *I* do. Trust me when I say that we need to proceed with baby steps." Her mouth kicks up. "Otherwise you may be the one who ends up living in Iowa."

"I hear Iowa's great," I tease then add when I see the protest growing on her face, "I'm not in any hurry to share you with the rest of the world, gorgeous. So long as you're in my arms every night, I'll wait as long as you want before we take on Dubois."

THIRTY-FIVE

Marie

BEYOND LATE BECAUSE my morning chat and cuddle with Jace turned into a morning lovefest that ended with both of us naked and me experiencing three glorious orgasms to his one, I hustle through the door toward my boss, my head spinning with details and excitement.

Because Attie was excited by what I found too.

Because we're closing in.

Fucking *finally*.

"Jace," Jean-Michel says, pushing out of his chair and moving toward us, hand extended for Jace to shake. "Just a second," he tells him before turning to me and taking my arm.

God, my heart squeezes, my boss is such a good guy.

And I'm so glad he found a woman who finally appreciates all of that goodness.

But when he starts to guide me from his office, likely intending to give me privacy, I dig in my heels and say, "No." I nod at Jace. "Mr. Henderson is the reason we found the connection."

Jean-Michel frowns, blue eyes flicking between Jace and me. "What connection?"

I open my mouth. Close it. Unsure where to start.

Thankfully, Jace bails me out.

"Duarte tried to fuck us over too," he says, handing over the stack of papers I pulled together last night. Jean-Michel's frown deepens as he starts quickly flipping through them—contracts, emails, and—

I watch him go still.

And I know why—both the Lyon family and Angela's name are all over those papers. The real estate company, the Duarte contract, the security reports, the scientist at Genen-core.

It's concrete evidence of her connection with the trafficking ring that Agent Phillips has been trying so hard to bring down.

Speaking of—

"I called Attie," I tell him. "And she's coming down to talk while her team heads to Mr. Henderson's office." There's excitement in my voice, so much so that I can practically feel it bubbling through my insides.

Or maybe that's just because I'm next to Jace.

Champagne in my veins. Hope in my heart. Love in my—

I jerk my gaze away from Jace.

He's wearing another suit that is temptation personified, and I'm having a hard time keeping my professional focus.

Hard to do when I want to launch myself in his arms and lick him all over.

Focus.

"Suzanne and I have been looking for a connection between all of this," I tell him, "and we finally have one that will actually pay off—"

"Roll this back for me," Jean-Michel says, not meanly, but

deliberately. And I know I have the luxury of yesterday, of talking it through with Jace to make sense of the loose ends. "Last I heard," he says, "all we had proof of was her bugging the shit out of me and fucking with our contracts. It's bad news that she's doing that shit with other companies"—he flicks his eyes to Jace's—"sorry she's being a pain in the ass for you too."

Jace shrugs.

"But unless I've missed something, I don't see anything that connects her to something bigger."

I frown.

It's there.

It makes perfect sense and—

"That's because you didn't see this," Jace says, snagging the stack of papers and flicking through them, pulling one out and showing Jean-Michel—

"Fuck," he hisses.

I exhale. Because I know it's the defense contract, which along with the other paperwork...provides the connection between Angela and the Lyon family that the FBI has been searching for.

"She was this fucking dumb?" he says, and I know what he's thinking. His ex-wife has been slippery and smart, impossible to pin down.

Until now.

"Dumb or not," I say, "it'll be enough to hold her, and it should be enough to persuade her to go the fuck away and stop bothering us, especially with the FBI on her ass."

Jean-Michel doesn't look completely convinced, but at least he's nodding.

"Your ex has been a pain in my ass for months now," Jace tells him, an intense scowl marring the beautiful lines of his face.

"Tell me about it," Jean-Michel mutters.

"But," Jace goes on, moving close to me, "if opening my doors to the FBI means I can run my business without her trying to burn shit down from the inside out then, like I told Marie, I'm open to it."

Jean-Michel nods. "Appreciated."

"I know that you're both busy," I say, gathering the papers up. I can feel the heat of Jace's body, can smell the spicy scent of him, and his closeness makes it a struggle to focus.

I'll punish him later for his insolence.

A breath.

Then I focus and turn to face him, looking up into dancing hazel eyes. He knows exactly what he's doing to me, especially after he fucked me senseless on his desk last night.

Something that's not helping me concentrate.

I shake myself, lift my chin. "I'll liaise with Attie's team and your company, Mr. Henderson. I'll make sure we follow this to ground, and hopefully it'll pan out as we expect." I pull out a pen, a pad of paper, and glare at him for a moment before glancing down at my pad.

It's either that or stab him with my pen.

Or kiss him and all this playing it cool stuff will go out the window.

"Who's the best person to coordinate with this on at Genen-core?" I ask archly.

He doesn't miss a beat. "Me."

I blink, feel my cheeks get hot.

He reaches into his pocket, passes me a card...and it has the stink's cell phone number on it.

I can't wait to spam the shit out of it.

Or maybe sell it on the black market.

"I need to run to another meeting," he murmurs, those dancing hazel eyes holding mine. "Call me anytime."

Then he's gone.

"Something you need to tell me?" Jean-Michel asks quietly.

Yes! Fucking yes.

But...one problem at a time. "No."

"Marie," he warns.

I carefully pocket the card, weigh how much to tell this good man, this *overprotective* man. I settle on, "We met a few months back. I didn't know who he was, and he tried to take my Lyft." I snag the papers, stack them carefully, taking my time and making sure each of the four edges is carefully aligned. "We had words." A shrug. Another sigh as I fumble with my words. "And now he's here."

He falls quiet, studying me for a long moment, and I'm *this* close to spilling my guts when he releases me from that intense stare and says, "Tiff is waiting, and I need to get home to her. Do you need me here for this?"

"No," I say, probably far too eagerly before I settle myself and add, "It's the same as before—keep your distance, I'll update you with what you need to know, and hopefully that'll keep you well away from any investigation fallout and future court dates."

"Let's hope those court dates for her aren't all that far into said future."

I smile as he leaves, but I know it's distracted.

Because I have the weight of that card in my pocket.

And because I know that Jace will be waiting for me to use it.

Same as he'll be waiting for me tonight.

No matter how late I get home.

THIRTY-SIX

Jace

"JEAN-MICHEL KNOWS SOMETHING'S UP," she says, nose wrinkled adorably.

It's been several weeks since Marie came to my office that night and all Agent Phillips has told her and me is that the FBI is working on putting the pieces together.

Seriously.

I may call her Attie, just to spur her into motion.

And in the meantime, we're supposed to continue as usual.

Not the easiest thing in the world for the two control freaks currently occupying the bed in her condo deal with, and I know that Marie is struggling with the same itchy, powerless feelings as me.

But there's nothing to be done and work has been insane for both of us—me trying hard to get the endometriosis treatment back on the calendar. It's not looking promising, as we're still fighting the patent shenanigans which is forcing us to jockey projects around on the schedule to make certain we have all our ducks in a row. Add in needing to hire another security company, one who can work to make the campus safe for my employees without tipping off the Duarte subsidiary...and then, theoretically the other, more powerful players Agent Phillips is working to take down, and I've barely had time to spend with Marie.

Thankfully, my woman had an in with a man named Pascal and connected us.

His company will be covering Genen-core until we can move forward with his recommendation for a corporate security firm.

And Marie has been just as busy on her end, though it has less to do with scheduling and security and the FBI, and more to do with Jean-Michel.

Because he's been busy taking care of the woman he loves.

And she's been taking on more responsibilities than normal.

Even still, the man is too smart to miss that something's changed with his righthand woman, even if she keeps putting him off.

"We talked about this, cookie," I say. "He won't miss what's happening between us for long."

"I know," she murmurs. "I just...I want him to enjoy this pause, to enjoy being with Tiff, and not worry about me."

Sassy and stubborn and *sweet*.

"I get that, cookie. But eventually he's going to come out of his love haze."

"Is he, though?"

I tug a curl. "Yes, gorgeous," I say, but soften it with a smile. "Still, it's your choice and"—I cup her jaw, hold her eyes with my own—"if there are other things at play here, things that make you feel like you want to take this slower, then I'm doubly okay with that."

She frowns. "If I want to take this slower?"

"Things have been pretty intense between us since that night at my office. If the reason that you don't want to go public with us is because it's been too fast—"

"No." She clambers on top of me, hands coming to my cheeks, eyes filled with an intensity that soothes the ache inside me, the worry I hadn't really acknowledged was starting to eat at me. "*No*," she says then snags her phone from the nightstand. "I'll call him right now, handsome. I'll tell him every detail—well, not *every* detail—but enough that he knows exactly how strongly I feel about you so he won't stage a corporate takeover and reduce Genen-core to its requisite parts."

I grin, take her phone from her hand, and toss it on the nightstand. "How is it that you talking about a corporate takeover is the height of romance?"

Pink cheeks. "I didn't—"

"Cookie," I say, drawing her down on top of me. "You just said that you like me, *really* like me. You can't take that back now."

"Jace—"

"Nope," I tease. "I have it on record now." Her nose wrinkles and it's so fucking cute that I can't stop my next words. "Don't worry, gorgeous, I like you, *really* like you too."

Her inhale is sharp. "Jace."

Big emotions. Big fears. Baby steps.

But I know for sure that she's worried about Jean-Michel because she cares about this, about *us*. So, I can be patient. Can go slowly. Can enjoy the fact that even though I don't have her out in the real world, I have her here. In my bed or hers, falling asleep beside her, waking up with her in my arms.

The rest will come.

"When is your flight tomorrow?" I ask when she sighs and settles against me.

"Early," she says on a yawn, that nose wrinkling again. "But that means we'll beat the time change by getting into NYC so we have a full day with the team."

"You'll wake me before you go?"

"Handsome," she begins, pushing up, "you have a long day tomorrow." She's not wrong about that. I'm meeting with the board in the evening and that's going to take a full day of prep on top of my normal responsibilities. "I'll call you when we land and it's a reasonable hour here."

I study her face, wanting to argue.

Then decide that's a battle I'm not going to win, not tonight anyway.

And pressing this is just going to cut further into her sleep.

I slide my hand into her hair, gently coax her back down onto my chest. "Okay, gorgeous. You win."

She kisses my chest. "Victory is mine."

Laughing, I ask her more about her day, answer when she asks me about mine, and when the yawns start coming with ever-growing frequency, I say, "Want to hear how Brooks and I first met?"

"Oh, my God, yes!"

So clearly, that interest has the opposite effect of what I intended—to soothe her into sleep—because as I relate how Brooks and I were college roommates and my first meeting with him involved him naked...though not because he was with a woman she's amused.

Then outraged.

"Those jerks!"

"Yeah," I agree. "The other guys on the floor were complete dicks. He'd just wanted a shower and they stole his clothes and towel, locked him out of our room." I chuckle because it's funny now. "He was covered up—but in the, no pun intended, barest sense of the word. Because the only thing he had was a loofa and it wasn't covering much."

"Poor guy."

"I'd agree with you if we weren't in a coed dorm and that little stunt meant that he never spent a night alone unless he wanted too."

"My poor handsome guy," she says softly, though her eyes dance. "Were you jealous?"

"Nah. He was a good wingman."

She pops me lightly on the chest. "Rude."

I kiss the tip of her nose. "No, what was rude was me not having a solid night's sleep until we moved to an off-campus apartment our junior year and I got my own room."

She asks a hundred questions about Brooks, about my college years, wants a thousand details I never even thought about, even shares a few of her own that I soak up like the gems they are. But eventually my plan begins to work.

Her yawns come with more regularity.

Her body relaxes fully against mine.

Her breaths even out.

She falls asleep on top of me.

And I hold her close like the precious gift she is.

THIRTY-SEVEN

Marie

MY BODY DOESN'T KNOW what time zone I'm supposed to be in, but I'm walking into my office anyway.

I've been traveling for three days straight, and while I normally would make a long weekend out of my last stop—especially since it was in central London, one of my favorite places on the planet—I took the company jet back to California.

Because Jace is home.

Because I've turned into a sappy woman who wants to be close to my boyfriend, who misses him with what might have been alarming intensity if not for the fact that he made it clear he misses me just as much.

Texts and FaceTime calls. A delivery of dinner from my favorite Covent Garden restaurant to my hotel room when I mentioned our flight was delayed and I wouldn't be able to make it out before they closed. Talking me down from the edge of panic when Jean-Michel finally had enough of me saying nothing is different and demanded that we talk the moment I get home...and then arranging for a masseuse to come up to my room and give me the best facial and massage of my life.

Jace showing me he can be thoughtful, even from five thousand miles away.

Showing me again that he's not like the other men.

That he's one of the good ones—like Jean-Michel.

Thank God for stubborn protective green flags, huh?

So, even though my bones are weary and my inbox is overflowing, every cell in my body itchy to skip these few hours in the office to catch up and meet with Jean-Michel, I see that his thoughtfulness continues.

Because there is a huge display of flowers on my desk.

My favorites, irises, are included, even though I swear I've never disclosed that fact to this man.

I stand there, admiring them for a moment.

They're big and bold and beautiful, so much like what I feel for him.

Then I process where they're sitting.

And what it means.

Jean-Michel knows something is up, I'm meeting with him in—I check my watch—twenty minutes, and there's a giant arrangement of flowers taking up most of my desk.

"Crap," I whisper, shoving my phone back in my pocket.

I'd pulled it out, intending to text Jace, to thank him.

But now I kind of want to throttle him.

I hurry over to the bouquet, reaching for the ornate glass vase, and freeze, noticing the envelope with my name scrawled on the front.

In Jace's handwriting.

Which means he went down to the florist himself, that he wrote the note inside. Not an online order or something his assistant took care of for him.

He'd done it himself.

My heart goes pitter-patter, and I snag the envelope out of the plastic fork thingy that's holding it in place then tear it open.

Yup. Definitely Jace's handwriting.

A fact that makes my pulse speed up...and that's even before I process the words on the little card.

To deepest, darkest secrets. And your ability to take their power away.

—J

P.S. *I talked to JM yesterday. Handled the worst of the inquiry. But he's going to want details from you too, cookie.*

Thud.

My heart collides against my rib cage, and I don't know how to handle the swell of emotions in my chest.

Mostly because every time I think that Jace can't get more wonderful, he does.

"So it's like that, huh?"

I turn, see that Jean-Michel has walked into my office without me noticing.

His mouth tips up. "Yeah, kid," he says, answering for me. "I can see it's like that."

"I don't know what you're thinking," I begin. "But—"

"You and Jace have been seeing each other for weeks now, Marie," he says, slipping by me and leaning back against my desk. "Is there a reason you didn't think to mention it?"

"I didn't want to step on what you and Tiff are building," I tell him.

"That may be part of it." He lightly touches one of the flowers, glances down at the torn-open envelope, and I clutch the note with Jace's precious words a little tighter to my chest. "But it's not all of it."

"You're overloaded with all the nonsense that Angela created—"

"Not anymore. You saw to that, and Attie is just tying up loose ends."

"—and Tiff has enough trouble on her plate, not to mention Chrissy being pregnant and Rory getting hitched, for real this time." I pocket the note, round my desk, and sink down into my chair, mostly so the spray of flowers hides me as I add, "Plus, you've got work responsibilities and contract negotiations and—"

"Excuses, kid." He picks up the flowers, carries them to the window sill, setting them down with a careful *clink*. Then, shield taken away from me, he's back in front of my desk, eyes locked onto mine.

I try to hold out.

Or come up with something that doesn't sound pathetic.

Unfortunately, all I manage is, "I didn't want you to worry."

He sighs, sits down in the chair across from me. "That's what Jace said when he came by to talk to me, and I'm not calling you a liar. All those things you and he mentioned are part of the truth, but I know you well enough to get they're not everything. Same as I think that Jace knows that too."

My pulse speeds.

Then there's nothing to it, the words just slip out. "I like him, JM. Like him more than I've ever liked another man." Maybe I even love him—a thought that has my heart stutter-starting again. "But you know my track record better than anyone: I'm shit at picking men. It's why I resisted giving him the time of day in the first place, even though he made it clear he was interested."

"Something obviously changed."

"Mostly that he was too damned stubborn to take no for an answer."

Jean-Michel's lips curve.

"Not that *you* know anything about that," I mutter, knowing that his first meeting with Tiff wasn't exactly the stuff of fairytales.

More like kidnapping fantasies with a morally gray hero.

"But I found I didn't want to say no, and then I found the more time I spent with him, the more I realized he wasn't like the other men." I scowl. "Which is even fucking scarier."

"You wouldn't have a reason to keep him at a distance."

I nod. "Nope."

"So, now what?"

"What do you mean?"

"Now what are you going to do? Keep that hand up so you can fend him off? Or give in and see where things take you?"

"I think I dropped my hand a while ago," I whisper. "Because even with it up, I didn't have any hope of keeping him out of my heart."

Jean-Michel smirks. "Sucks, huh?"

"Sucks so bad it's the best thing I've ever had in my life."

Now his face goes soft and he reaches forward, takes my hand. "That's half the battle."

"Not being a chicken shit?"

He laughs. "Damn straight. Just channel your negotiating Marie and power through the scary parts."

"The worst thing is that Jace seems to know when I'm scared and I don't even have to go that far. I can just be me because he's got his hand out, ready to haul me safely to the other side."

"Fuck, kid."

"What?" I whisper.

"I wanted to keep channeling some hate for the bastard."

My brow furrows. "I thought you liked him."

"I do," he says. "But you—not him—have a piece of my heart."

I sniff. "Tiff's made you sappy."

"No," he says. "She just helped me see the beauty around me." I sniff again and he pushes up from his chair. "All right. Enough of this. Time for you to call it a day." He grabs my bag, my coat, and moves to the door. "And I don't want to see you here tomorrow, either."

"But—"

He pulls open the door, shoves my stuff into my arms, and orders, "Go home, kid."

I'm nearing the elevators when I hear my name and turn back.

"You know what this means, right?" he calls.

I shake my head, eyebrows dragging together. "No."

"You're both expected at family dinner Saturday."

THIRTY-EIGHT

Jace

"WHY DO I feel like I'm about to be dragged down into the hills and made into a human scarecrow?" I mutter as I open Marie's door and help her out of the car.

She grins up at me. "Probably because of the trio of giant hockey players currently gathered on the porch glaring at you?"

I tap the tip of her nose. "Got it in one."

Her hand finds mine. "It'll be fine, handsome. They look scary and they can obliterate six-foot-six, two-hundred-and-twenty-pound guys on the ice but—"

"Not helping, cookie."

A giggle and I can't lie, *that* helps.

That she can laugh and joke with me, that her fingers are wrapped tightly around mine, that she leans into me as we walk. That when we pause to climb the couple of steps up onto the porch at Jean-Michel's daughter, Chrissy's, house, she tugs me to a stop, rises on tiptoe, and presses a kiss to my jaw. "I can handle a couple of hockey players." She winks. Then tugs me forward again. "Trust me."

"I do."

She stills for a heartbeat then her eyes are flashing to mine over her shoulder.

Our gazes only lock for a moment but the intensity of emotions in hers takes my breath away.

Then she's looking forward, drawing me alongside her, and saying in a stage whisper, "And Jean-Michel has the money, power, and connections to bankrupt you, even despite the *large*"—a smile in my direction that has my dick twitching at a seriously inopportune time—"size of your bank account."

"Cookie," I warn.

The pregnant brunette grins and steps forward, unceremoniously pushing the hockey players and Jean-Michel to the side. "Hi"—she extends a hand—"I'm Chrissy." We shake. "And I know you know my dad, Jean-Michel. This is Rome, my fiancé." A nudge to the brown-haired man who tugs her back against his chest. "And my best friend, Rory." I've barely noticed the blonde, she's so dwarfed by the huge, bearded man who has her tucked close to his side. "Her husband, King. And I think you know Attie—"

A cough from the curly-haired brunette.

"Er, Ats," she corrects with a smile at the other woman. "I think you two have met?"

I nod, reach out and shake Agent Phillips's hand. "We have. Nice to see you again."

"Cam," I hear and glance over at the thinnest of the trio of hockey players. He has a possessive edge to his expression and hovers close to Attie—but doesn't attempt to crush my fingers when we shake hands. "Jace," I say.

"Good." Chrissy claps her hands together. "Now that that's

all out of the way, let's go inside. The food's going to get cold and this baby is hungry."

"Meow!"

I turn toward the pretty gray tabby on the cat tower. "Hey, gorgeous," I say softly, reaching a hand out—

Then freezing when the rest of the occupants of the kitchen yell, "No!"

"Um," I begin.

Chrissy takes a step toward me. "Joan of Freaking Arc. My cat," she explains when my brows drag together. "She's not, well...nice."

But even as she says that, a furry head rubs against my still outstretched hand.

Then the soft rumble of a purr.

I lightly stroke her head then grunt when she launches herself from the cat tower and into my arms. Holding her carefully, I turn back to the others, the remains of the dinner—pizza and pasta from a local Italian place named Mario's—littered on the huge island.

Bar stools are pushed back, half-full glasses of wine are dotted around.

Cats and dogs run underfoot, visitors from Rory and Chrissy's animal rescues, and Tiff, Jean-Michel's other half, who arrived late from her job, is just diving into a plate he made up for her.

An ice cream cake—Chrissy's craving today—is thawing on the counter, and I think that could take a solid hour and I would still be too full for a slice.

I'll still eat one anyway—because I've never had this special concoction from Molly's.

And it looks fucking incredible.

But none of that explains why the entire kitchen full of people is now looking at me like I've grown a second head.

Rome is the first to break out of his shock.

He chuckles and shakes his head, muttering, "Joan of Freaking Arc."

"I don't get it," I say, stroking a hand through her soft fur.

"She's surly and will bite your head off if you move wrong," King explains.

I glance down at the ball of fluff in my arms. Joan stares up at me through half-slit eyes, her purrs vibrating through my chest. "Surly?" I ask disbelievingly.

"With those she judges as unworthy," Marie says, coming close to my side and reaching forward to scratch the cat. "Which clearly"—a pointed look up at me—"you are not."

I touch her cheek. "And neither are you."

A sigh has my head jerking up, Joan's purring faltering for a moment.

Chrissy's smiling at us, and the looks of murder the guys have been wearing all night have evened out. But it's Jean-Michel's expression that's changed the most.

He nods at me, approval evident.

"Meow?"

I look down at Joan. "Did I stop scratching you?"

"Meow."

We all laugh. I go back to scratching, earning that persistent purring for several minutes before Joan decides she's had enough. Her teeth, sharp pinpricks of bright white canines, press lightly into my hand.

"Yes, darling?" I ask her.

Her teeth press a little harder.

I get the message and settle her back onto her perch, where she can look down her adorable nose at us.

Marie slides closer, wrapping her arm around my waist as we wander back to the island, listening to the guys chatter about their upcoming games and as Rory and Chrissy discuss her plans for her upcoming baby shower. We chime in when necessary—and it's fairly frequent because they're all good at including us in the conversation—but I'm enjoying just standing on the sidelines, watching their interactions.

Friendship and love.

New acquaintances and old.

But it's comfortable, enjoyable...and it's Marie's.

I'm glad she has it, grateful I'm here to be part—however small—of it.

We stay until Chrissy starts yawning and Rome ushers us out the door. I drive us home, and it doesn't take long for Marie to fall asleep. I don't wake her, just carry her sleeping form up to my condo, tucking her into my bed and pulling the covers up and over her.

I lock up, plug in our phones.

Then crawl in beside her, tugging her against me.

As sleep starts to claim me, I can't help but think this was the best night I've had in a long time.

Because of Marie.

And because Chrissy made me promise that next time I bring Brooks along.

He won't know what hit him.

My lips curve.

Fall into the blackness.

And when I wake up in the morning and my Marie is gone, I'm not upset.

Because there's an envelope on the table...with Eagles tickets inside.

Her note alongside them makes me laugh.

They're not playoff tickets, but I still want snacks.

-M

THIRTY-NINE

Marie

"I HAVE to say I like your outfit from Dean's better."

I jump, starting to turn, but I don't get far before Jace is slipping his arms around me, his chest pressing to my back.

Male and spice and *mine*.

"You don't like me sporting an Eagles jersey?"

"No," he murmurs, lips pressing to the sensitive spot behind my ear. "I just like a short, backless dress, with sexy underwear beneath it better than jeans and a hockey jersey."

I spin in his hold, throw my arms around his neck, our bodies flush, desire blooming in my belly. "Would it help if I told you that I'm wearing sexy underwear tonight too?"

"It would definitely help." He draws me closer, takes the chance to slant his lips over mine, not releasing me until my knees are shaking and I'm ready to blow off the game altogether. "We should go in, gorgeous. We need time to get your snacks before puck drop."

My nose wrinkles, and he grins, taking my hand and drawing me toward the metal detectors in front of the arena.

"Would it help if you told me all the food you want me to buy for you?"

I grin. "Maybe."

He passes over the tickets to be scanned, ushers me ahead of him. "Definitely popcorn."

"Absolutely." I step inside when the security guard waves me forward. "And Swedish fish."

"Huh?"

"What?" I ask, glancing back over my shoulder at him.

"I would have thought you'd be a KitKat girl."

"Oh, that's on my list too," I say. "Along with nachos and Buncha Crunch and a hot dog and—"

He stops, eyes going wide as they drag down and up my body.

It's not like when he's eating me up with his gaze, his desire burning into me.

It's...shock.

"You're serious?"

I stop, brow furrowing. "If it's too much, I can buy my own snacks, handsome."

"I—" A shake of his head. "Obviously I can afford your snacks. Hell, cookie, I could buy everyone in here their snacks and not see a difference in my bank account. It's just..."

"Just what?

"Where the hell do you put it?"

"I'm sorry?"

"That's enough junk food for an entire hockey team, and you're the size of my pinky finger, so"—he tugs at a curl—"where the hell do you put it, gorgeous?"

I swat his chest lightly, open my mouth to demand my

snacks, but then I see Jean-Michel rushing out of the area where the owner's suites are. "What the—?"

"What is it?" Jace asks, teasing immediately leaving his tone.

"I just saw Jean-Michel—" I look again, but I've lost him in the crowd. "His face—"

"What?" he asks, and I realize I haven't finished the sentences, too lost in looking for my boss.

"Worried, I guess."

I pull out my phone, but there aren't any missed calls or texts from my boss. "I—"

Jace cups my jaw then brushes his lips over my forehead. "I'll grab snacks. You go check on him."

My heart squeezes. "I'm sure it's fine. He'll call me if he needs—"

"Cookie." My eyes go to his. "Go."

I debate for one more second before I lift up on tiptoe and brush my lips over his. "Thank you."

He presses my ticket into my hand and then he's turning for the concession stand.

I hurry over to the box, greet the security guard by name—because as much as I don't enjoy watching hockey, I know all of Jean-Michel's security staff. "Is everything okay?"

He nods, and I push inside the owner's suite, finding Chrissy and Rory inside.

And...then everything goes to hell.

THE NEXT HOUR IS A MESS.

A complete and total mess that ends up with me having to talk to another FBI agent—and this time it's not just Attie, er Agent Phillips.

Because it's agents, plural.

Because when it's all said and done, Tiff, *Jean-Michel's Tiff*, is caught up in the overflow of the FBI investigation into Angela Rosseau, Duarte, corporate espionage, and kidnapping and trafficking. Complete and total insanity that threatens almost everything Jean-Michel holds dear.

But Tiff...I exhale slowly.

She's a survivor.

And Attie's team is watching.

They get to Tiff in time.

But, unfortunately, Angela slips through the FBI's defenses and has disappeared.

Again.

We're all disappointed and frustrated—and terrified for Tiff.

Thankfully, she's unharmed and she drags Jean-Michel back into the light. *Literally.* She survives a close call, calms him down, and then literally drags him back upstairs, just in time for puck drop.

And I remain below, handling the fallout, liaising with the investigative team, trying to handle everything so that Jean-Michel can just worry about Tiff and himself.

It works.

I get the corridors blocked off and the security footage to Attie. I keep the press and players and staff away...and in doing so, I don't so much as look at my phone.

And *I* don't make it up for puck drop.

And I don't tell Jace what's happening.

I just left him—

"Shit," I whisper, drawing the attention of several agents. Attention that really isn't smart, considering what happened here tonight. "Sorry," I say, hurrying down the hall and yanking my phone from my pocket.

Seeing a series of texts on the screen.

> JACE: You good, cookie?

> JACE: Text me and let me know all's fine when you get a chance, okay?

> JACE: The second period is about to start and I'm getting a little worried, gorgeous. Can you check in?

> JACE: I just saw Jean-Michel. He explained. Take your time.

> JACE: I know you're in the zone, cookie. Take care of what you need to take care of then crawl into bed beside me when you're done.

I still, my eyes burning, guilt rippling through me.

Because it dawns on me then.

That our whole relationship could be this, like tonight, like the last weeks have been—Jace taking care of me if only I let him in. Which, on the surface, doesn't seem bad. The problem is that he does it without a second thought.

And I'm so used to protecting myself that I might not think of him, not in the same way he does for me.

Our relationship could be him looking out for me, bending for me, working his ass off to give me *exactly* what I want, his needs be damned. And he could be—not exactly forgotten like he was with all that complicated his and his mom's relationship —but also not on the receiving end of the same care and affection as he gives to me.

It's such a searing, painful realization that I know I need to do better.

To make sure he knows he's seen.

That he's not forgotten.

That...I love him.

Wherever you are feels like home.

I take a deep breath, make a promise to the universe and myself, and let go of my deepest darkest secret.

I finally picked right.

And I think I know exactly how to show Jace how much I love him.

So, even though I know she's insanely busy after the events of tonight, I walk down the hall and wave down Attie.

"You're good to go," she says. "We'll be wrapped up here in the next half hour."

"That's great. I just..." I falter, nerves me gripping tightly.

Her head tilts to the side, brown curls bouncing. "What is it?"

I push through my fear and say, "I need a favor."

FORTY

Jace

"DUDE," Brooks mutters a month later.

"What?" I say, eyes flicking from the screen up to my friend's.

"Whipped."

I punch his shoulder, but take the grumpy *dude* as how it's intended and pocket my phone. "I'll remind you that you're the one who gave me the shove to pursue things with Marie."

"So I did." He lifts his beer bottle to his lips and drinks deeply. "Of course, I didn't think I'd be sharing every meal with her."

I'd get in his face if he meant those words.

But I can see his eyes, see they're filled with devilry. And I know him well enough to understand when he's just trying to piss me off.

Well, he's succeeding.

"When are you heading back to France again?" I grumble.

Because it's tradition.

"Nice try," he mutters, picking up the remote and turning on the Eagles playoff game. "But considering you've offered to help me unload my storage container after the game's done, you know that's a pointless question."

"Why did I agree to help you move again?"

"Because we're friends, and friends do that shit."

"And we're just ignoring the fact that both of us could buy a moving company ten times over so we don't *have* to do it ourselves?"

"Eh." He shrugs and polishes off his beer. "A little manual labor will do you good if you're bitching this much about a trunk's worth of boxes."

I scowl.

But because he's right, I don't comment further.

And by the time I polish off my beer, the Eagles have won, and we're getting into Brooks's SUV.

He turns out onto the street, starts winding his way through the rolling green hills, having moved into the exclusive community that abuts the Oak Ridge vineyards and estate. It's a nice area, and there are a few empty lots left.

Maybe I can convince Marie to build something from scratch.

Some place where we can progress our relationship.

Some place we can fill with memories and...kids.

Or maybe I need to slow my roll, because I've only just gotten her to the point she's comfortable with being my girlfriend.

I don't even know if she wants kids.

Scratching that on to my mental checklist to ask the next time I have an opportunity, I tune back into the winding roads and realize—

"Hey, this isn't the way to the storage—"

He pulls to a stop, glances over at me.

"That's because I'm not going to force you to load some boxes, dumbass." His mouth tips up. "But I'm damned glad you're willing to because I reserve the right to torture you with it another day."

I frown at him, having no clue what the fuck is going on. "I—"

Something he clearly sees. "Man, *look*."

Finally, I stop staring at him.

And I look, not processing what I'm seeing at first.

Marie is standing behind her car, watching us.

"What's—"

"Go to her," Brooks orders.

"You—" Another shake of my head. "She—"

"She needed someone to keep you busy for a few hours. Mission accomplished," he says quietly. "Now go enjoy whatever it is she has planned, yeah? And make sure you tell her how much you love her at the end of it."

"I—"

But I don't tell him to mind his own business or that I don't love her.

Because Brooks is right.

She's mine, and my heart is hers...and it's been that way since she first stole my Lyft.

I pop the door, climb out, pausing before I throw it closed. "Brooks?"

I don't miss the shadows in his eyes.

Or the way he quickly tucks them away. "Yeah?"

"Thanks," I say. "For everything."

He nods. I close the door.

And then I'm walking toward the woman I love.

Vaguely, I hear him turn his car around and drive off. But it's a distant thought because every cell in my body is focused on the woman in front of me.

"Hey," she murmurs when I get close enough to take her hand.

"Hey, cookie," I say, drawing her against me. "Why the subterfuge?"

"Because I needed to give you something."

"What's that, gorgeous?"

She passes me an envelope.

"What's this?"

"Open it."

Confused, but intrigued, I tear open the flap, pull out the paper, not processing what I'm reading at first.

Because it doesn't make sense.

"I had Attie pull some strings," she whispers. "Turns out her boss knew someone in the patent office. She managed to fast track your application."

I can't believe what I'm looking at.

Can't begin to process it.

"You did this for me?"

"It was nothing, handsome," she says. "And really, it was Attie who did most of the work."

"It was you." I carefully fold the paper, tuck it in my pocket, then I move closer to Marie and cup her face gently in my hands. "Thank you for opening up that gorgeous heart to me. You can't know what it means—"

"I do."

Of course she does.

Because this—us—means just as much to her.

"Still," I whisper. "Thank you."

Her smile is so beautiful, it takes my breath away. "I'm the one who should be thanking *you*."

"Let's keep arguing about it for the rest of our lives, yeah?" I tease.

"I'd like that very much," she whispers, sending my pulse

skyrocketing because the sincerity in her tone is almost blindingly intoxicating. And I know it's because she's finally allowed herself to be mine. "I, um," she murmurs. "I also had Brooks bring you here because I wanted to show you something."

I'm not sure I can handle anything else, but still, I say, "What's that, cookie?"

She shifts, jerking her chin behind me. "That."

I frown, turn around, and I can't process it at first, what I'm seeing. "I—" I clear my throat, trying my best to speak normally when my heart is thudding so hard against my ribs that the beats feel like physical blows, when my pulse is thrumming through my ears so loudly it's making it hard to concentrate enough to form words. "H-how?" I rasp out. "Wh-why?"

Because it's *all* I can get out.

Because behind me is an empty lot. And a realtor sign.

And perched on top of that sign is a smaller placard.

That reads...

SOLD.

"I know it's a big step, a crazy step," she says, her words rushing out in rapid succession. "But you mentioned that you liked that Brooks moved up here, and I've always loved it here too, always thought it would be nice to live near Chrissy and the others." She nibbles at her lip, worry crawling into her eyes. Probably because I can't summon any words and am just staring at her like an idiot. "So, I know this is stupid soon and probably insane, but I thought that maybe we could build something—a home—together. That we could maybe build it here."

I open my mouth.

Close it.

Then open it again.

And then...I can't stand it.

So, I turn on my heel and walk away.

FORTY-ONE

Marie

I FEEL as though my heart is going to shatter when he turns and walks away.

I can't believe I've been so wrong about this situation.

That I've fucked up so huge.

That he's just like the—

I freeze.

Drop into a crouch, my hands coming to the sides of my head, diving into my hair.

Because...he's just like the others.

God, he's just like the others.

My lungs hitch, my sobs almost escaping.

I can't let him see.

I *can't*.

I need to get out of here. I need—

Hands on top of mine, carefully pulling them away from my face.

"What's the matter, cookie?" Jace murmurs, and I can't look at him, can't feel him this close. Not when—

I pull my hands free, brush at my face. "It's nothing," I whisper, turning my head away.

There's a long pause. Then, "Why are you crying, gorgeous?"

God, it hurts when he calls me that.

When his reaction was—

I close my eyes.

And he doesn't want—

The pain in my chest is so intense that it takes my breath away, that my eyes glass over again, that my lungs struggle to work.

"Marie."

God. Why does his voice have to be so gentle?

Why does that gentle make all of this hurt so much?

"Cookie, just—"

"I'm fine." I stand, turn for my car. "I should go."

He snags my arm, stopping me before I can escape.

I can't look at him, not when my heart is breaking into a million pieces.

So, I just say again, "I should go."

He rocks back on his heels, as though I've wounded him. "You're going to do this"—he touches his pocket, where he'd so carefully stowed the patent approval—"and that"—a wave of his hand toward the land I'd so insanely purchased—"and you're just going to leave?"

"I-it's o-okay," I sputter. "I know that this was a dozen steps too far. Don't worry. I'm sure I can cancel the contract or resell the land. I—"

"Resell the land?" He scowls then moves forward, forcing me to skitter back, not stopping until he's pinned me between his body and my car. "Cancel the contract? What the fuck are you talking about, gorgeous?"

"You don't want this," I say. "I get it. Too much too soon. And—"

"Did I say I don't want this?"

It's a dry question, one that stops the cracking of my heart, sending confusion ricocheting through me in its wake. "No," I say, starting to come back to myself. "But then again, you didn't say anything. You just walked away."

He smiles, and it's so beautiful it takes my breath away. "You're right. I walked away. Because what you did with this" —another touch to his pocket—"and that"—another nod toward the sign—"are the nicest things that anyone has ever done for me." A beat. "*Ever.*"

"Jace," I begin.

"*Ever,*" he repeats. He cups my jaw, tilts my face up so our gazes are aligned. "And I love you for it."

Every cell in my body freezes and I rasp out, "What?"

"I love you, Marie. I have from the moment you aced me out of my own Lyft."

"I—" But I can't summon any other words.

That's okay, though. Because Jace is still talking.

"You know what I was thinking about when Brooks drove me over here?"

I shake my head.

"Nice play, by the way," he says, lightly running his thumb over my cheek, "getting my friend in on the action. I didn't suspect a thing."

"I'm sorry if I overstepped."

"Look at me, gorgeous. *Really* look at me."

I already am. I can't look away from him, can't tear my gaze from his beautiful emerald eyes.

"So, you know what I was thinking on the drive?"

I shake my head again.

"That I would love to buy a lot up here, love to build a house together, something that is *ours* alone."

My lungs inflate on a rush. "Really?"

His mouth curves up. "Yes, really."

"Oh."

"I'm in love with you, and the fact that you did this today, for me...I'm not running scared, cookie. I'm not leaving, not putting distance between us, not going to squander this opening you've given me into your heart." He bends and presses his lips to my forehead. "It's just..."

"What?" I ask breathlessly.

"I was overwhelmed because you just handed over the most priceless gift you could have given me."

"What's that?" I ask almost inaudibly. I know the patent is important to him because of all the hard work he's been doing, and the land wasn't cheap, but—

He crouches a little, holding my eyes when he says, "You."

I inhale sharply. "*Jace.*"

"I love you," he murmurs.

"I know," I say softly. I've felt it, held it close, found the strength to give it back.

"And now she goes and quotes *Star Wars* on me." A tug of my curl. "Could she be any more perfect?"

"You like *Star Wars?*" God, there are still so many things I'm learning about him.

But, for once, that doesn't make me scared.

Because, God, I can't wait to learn *everything* about him— from favorite movies all the way down to deepest darkest secrets.

Oh, wait. I already know those.

My heart's swelling with happiness at that realization when he teases, "I think you just bought yourself a movie marathon."

I groan, but I'm grinning. Because the original movies are

some of my favorite films of all times. A dashing, handsome Han Solo, a feisty and strong Princess Leia? How could I not love every bit of them?

They're Jace.

And me.

Us.

I touch his cheek. "So, you're not mad that I got Brooks to help me?" I ask. "Don't think I'm crazy about the property?"

"If you're crazy then you're in good company." He tugs a curl. "Because we're in it together."

"You know I love you too." It's another blurt.

And he smiles. "I know, cookie."

"And you're going to have to get used to it, you know?"

Now his eyebrows drag together. "Used to what?"

"Me taking care of you."

That frown deepens. "You don't need to do that."

"I know," I say. "And I don't care. You're thoughtful and sweet and stubborn as hell, and I love you. So, you just need to deal with me looking out for you. Besides," I add, "I know you'll be doing the exact same thing for me too."

His eyes are warm and soft and, God, I love him so much. "You're right."

"Ah," I tease, smoothing my hand along the stubble of his jaw. "My most favorite words of all time."

"Smart ass," he mutters, turning his head, pressing his lips against my palm.

"You like it."

"I do."

"And you know what else?"

"What's that, cookie?" he asks.

I lift on tiptoe, lean in so my lips are right at his ear. "I've got my sexy underwear on beneath this outfit too."

His eyes go hot.

His arms band tightly around me.

His lips drop to mine.

And, long minutes later, we pile into my car and head home to celebrate by taking our clothes—including the afore-mentioned underwear—off.

Turns out that Jace's is pretty sexy too.

And also that he was right all those weeks ago.

Home has become wherever we are together.

And that may be the most beautiful truth of all.

EPILOGUE

"I'M GOING to miss this place," she says quietly.

My head is in her lap and she's running her fingers through my hair, over and over again, nails scratching lightly against my scalp, the scent of flowers and *Marie* surrounding me.

"I am too," I say softly, looking around her now-empty condo.

We've ended up selling both of our places to the same man, a grumpy older billionaire that Jean-Michel knew was looking for a new place to live after his wife died. His name is Thorn Wilkenson, and he's as *thorny* as his name implies.

He's also grieving the loss of the woman he spent twenty years building a life wife.

And he needed a place to start over that wasn't filled with her memories.

So, he bought up both condos and is going to take over this entire floor.

But that means it's not going to be *our* place any longer —
not going to be the place where we started.

Which is fine, totally fine, because we've just finished
building our home. *Our* home. And it's amazing, beautiful,
ours. But it's not this place, not where we got our start, not the
beginning of us.

But...it can be the beginning of something else.

I slip my hand into my pocket, touch the edge of the
velvet-covered box I've been carrying around all day, and
hesitate.

Is this the right time?

Does she deserve something bigger and better and more
Instagram worthy?

Maybe I should do this at our new place, celebrate the
beginning of a new chapter of *us* there instead of the ending of
a previous one.

Maybe I should sweep her away to a private beach, get
down on one knee at sunset, pledge my heart to her forever.

Hell, maybe I should—

"The answer is yes, handsome."

My fingers spasm on the box. "What?"

"Well," she says, "scratch that..."

My heart spasms, words stoppering up in the back of my
throat. But before I can force them out, rasp out something that
resembles a proposal—or maybe a plea for her to take pity on
me and agree to be my wife—she keeps talking.

"My answer *will* be yes"—she shifts, nudging me up and
then onto my back before clambering on top of me—"if, and
only *if*, you"—she drags her hand down my front, fingers
drifting toward my suddenly hardening cock—"tell me why you
call me cookie."

Lips twitching, I settle my hands onto her hips. "I told you
already."

"About your dog named Cookie and our matching fur, er, hair?"

"Exactly."

A roll of those pretty eyes. "Or maybe you're talking about the time you told me it was because I had a chip on my shoulder, much like a chocolate chip cookie."

I snort, slip my fingers into the waistband of her pants.

"I believe I said much like Molly's peanut butter chocolate chip cookies," I correct, stroking lightly over her silky flesh.

A sigh. A droll look. "That's not any better."

"It's *significantly* better. Molly's cookies are your favorite."

"Jace," she warns.

And I can't resist sitting up and pressing my lips to hers for a short, blazing kiss.

"And..." she puffs out, "it's not because your favorite late-night sugary cereal is Cookie Crisps either." A beat. "So don't even try it."

I grin. "Okay, gorgeous. I won't."

"Okay, *cookie*," she says sternly.

"You really want to know?" I ask softly, touching her cheek.

"The hundred times I've asked over the last year haven't made it clear that I want to know?"

I chuckle. "Well, you're persistent."

"And so are you."

"Strong."

"Ditto."

"Well-dressed."

Her lips curve. "Right back at you, handsome."

"And," I murmur, cupping one cheek, "I took one look at you next to that Lyft and knew without a doubt that...you're a tough cookie."

She stills, mouth dropping open.

"But that's a bit of a mouthful," I tell her, sliding my free hand up along her spine, cupping the back of her head, allowing her curls to fall over my fingertips. "So…just cookie."

Her mouth opens.

Closes.

Her gorgeous eyes are watery pools of emeralds.

"Not that"—I lift up, nip lightly at her jaw—"you aren't tasty."

She laughs softly. "I can't believe it was so simple all this time."

"It popped in my head about two seconds after you browbeat me into not getting in the Lyft."

A wince. "Did I ever apologize for that?"

"Hmm." I press a row of kisses along the line of her jaw. "I'm not sure."

"I'm sorry, handsome." She turns her head, presses her mouth to mine, stealing my breath with a deep, searching kiss. "But I'm also not." She settles her forehead against mine. "Because it brought me you."

And that's when I know.

That this is the perfect moment.

I reach back into my pocket…and I pull out the box. "Marie Austen, will you—"

"Yes!"

Laughter bubbles up in my chest and I open the lid, slide the obscenely large diamond onto her finger (the better for the world to know she belongs to me). "Just to make it clear, since you didn't let me finish, I'm asking you to be my wife, not to make that delicious lasagna of yours again."

"And here I thought you just earned that for dinner tonight."

My stomach rumbles. "God, I love you."

"Right back at ya, handsome." She climbs to her feet,

extends a hand and draws me up to mine, her face going suddenly serious.

"What is it?" I ask.

"I love you."

"I know."

Her mouth curves. "And in honor of that," she says, "I think it's time we..."

I wait.

Brace myself.

And what she tells me after she draws me out into the hall, to the elevator, down to my car don't disappoint.

"Go home."

Yup. The most beautiful words a man can hear.

I take her hand, hold her stare with my own.

"I'm already there."

Brooks, Years Before

She's beautiful.

She's walking toward me in a wedding dress, crisp white and fitted in a way that mixes innocence and sin.

Sleek fabric clinging to breasts I've dreamed about, hips I've imagined grasping as I thrust deep, splitting on midthigh to give just a glimpse of silken skin.

Mine.

Mine.

The thought ricochets through me so violently, I know.

Know.

The truth.

The reality.

The...future.

But by the time I process it, what that reality means for my —*our*—future, she's there.

Her bright blue eyes glimmering with love and hope, with tears of happiness.

She...is beautiful and good and...

I'm a monster.

I'm going to destroy her.

Her hand finds mine and she steps close, fingers tightening in that soft way of hers, silently telling me she's here.

Her plump lips are painted pink. Her freckles are softened by her makeup. Her lashes look longer than normal, darkened with mascara, and they don't need help. They already rest gently on her cheeks when she sleeps.

"Dearly beloved we are gathered here today to..."

I nearly jump out of my skin at the soft female voice coming from between us. The officiant is holding a book even though it's clear she has her spiel memorized, even down to the timing of pauses, waiting for chuckles or laughter or whatever feedback she normally receives from a wedding ceremony.

But there aren't rows and rows of chairs, filled with loving family and friends.

There aren't many voices to lend their approval to the quiet jokes and idioms.

Just two stoic witnesses—one my bodyguard, who I trust with my life...and hers, and the other my best friend, Jace. Who I trust just as deeply.

The mountains are behind us.

A narrow swathe of pine trees surrounding us, their branches intertwining to form a canopy overhead.

It's a peaceful place.

Her place.

And I'm going to ruin that too.

Boom!

Thunder rattles through the air, vibrates through my chest, my stomach. It even shakes the pine needles overhead. Clouds gather, clinging together, darkening the sky. A darkness that is split by a sudden flash of lightning.

Fat, wet drops of rain began plopping to the ground, darkening the dirt, splattering onto my head, my suit.

Her dress.

Laughter in the air—and it's painful and beautiful all at once. Because the sound that so captivates me in this moment is also what has drawn me to this sweet, beautiful, *innocent* woman against every single reservation that I had.

It's not a sound I deserve to hear.

It's a sound I *won't* hear.

Not ever again.

Not after this.

Briar laughs as the drops began gathering on her skin like glittering diamonds.

The officiant stops, closes the book in her hands, glancing at them then up at the clouds. "Should we stop?"

"No!" Briar says again, slipping one hand from mine and extending it, droplets splashing onto her thumb. "I love the rain!" she cries, tilting her head back, embracing the drops as they fall onto her hair, darkening the blond strands, straightening the curls, soaking the fabric of her dress.

A pause from the officiant. Then she reopens her book.

Briar's eyes slide to mine, buoyant with joy. "This is perfect," she whispers as thunder booms again.

As lightning cuts across the sky.

As rain continues to fall.

Isn't it beautiful, Brooks? How the rain washes everything clean for a fresh start?

"Perfect," she whispers again, her damp palm coming to mine, fingers wrapping tight again.

No.

It isn't perfect.

It's my nightmare…and it will soon be hers too.

Because I'm going to ruin everything.

Before I can say something, can find the strength to pull my fingers from hers, the officiant continues.

"Do you, Brooks Saxton, take this woman to be your lawfully wedded wife, to live together in matrimony, to love her, comfort her, honor and keep her in sickness and in health, in sorrow and in joy, to have and to hold, from this day forward, as long as you both shall—"

"I don't."

The words are ripped from my soul.

Spat into the air.

Shock reverberates back.

From the officiant.

From the witnesses.

From *Briar*.

"I don't," I repeat.

Fingers convulse around mine. "You're supposed to say *I do*," Briar whispers.

My lungs seize. "No," I say. "I'm not."

"Brooks—"

I slip my hands from hers. It's not easy, not when she's clinging to me so fiercely. Not when she's looking at me like…

I can't allow that thought to form, can't allow the words to coalesce in my mind.

I might do something that's worse than this.

I might…stay.

"I don't," I say for a third time.

Though this time I pair it with putting distance between us, enough and so quickly that I see it break off a little chunk of that innocence, that sweetness, that essence that is purely Briar.

It falls to the side.

Gone.

Forever.

"You're supposed to say *I do*," Briar says again, more forcefully.

I shake my head, commit her ravaged face to memory, know I need to hold it tight, know it's the only memory of her I deserve.

Then I turn away. Turn from the sputtering of the officiant, turn from the shattering beauty.

I move toward Jace and Max. They've been with me from the beginning.

Long enough to not question anything.

"Max." I flick my eyes in the direction of Briar.

He nods...just as footsteps echo across the earth, louder than the rain, which is coming down in sheets now, drenching me, the earth.

Briar.

"Brooks!"

Max has been with me a long time.

Long enough to step behind me, to intercept Briar before she can touch me.

Because if she touches me, I may lose my resolve.

"Brooks!"

I start walking.

Keep walking.

Down along the narrow winding trail, the faint imprint in earthen ground that Briar knows by heart.

Her place.

Our place.

I keep walking...

Out of her life.

I think for forever.

Turns out, I'm wrong.

About so many things.

Briar, Present Day

I never thought I would be this person.

But...when it comes to the choice between doing something right and moral and surviving the next few months, I know I don't have any options.

Know I stopped having *choices* years ago.

On a rainy mountaintop that I thought would be the beginning of a happy life.

Instead, it became a nightmare.

My nightmare.

I adjust my gloves, knowing I can't risk leaving behind even a trace of evidence that I was here.

Hating that I *am* here with every fucking fiber of my being.

"Just suck it up and do it," I whisper. "Then you never have to face it again."

And I would *never* have to be here again.

I tug at my beanie, making sure it completely covers my silver blond hair. I used to love it, used to love the unique color, the way other people reacted to it, long and sleek and bright like moonlight.

I brushed it obsessively, carefully detangled each and every knot. Oiled the ends. Used a protective spray every single day. Slept only on silk pillowcases.

That stopped being my life on that mountaintop.

I let it get so bad, so matted and tangled, I had to cut it all off. Even now, I'm still growing out the unfortunate pixie style I ended up with.

And today, it's more nuisance than asset.

It's why I chopped the shoulder length tresses to above my chin, hacking away with a pair of rusty scissors I found in the dumpster behind the thrift store.

Sometimes the best stuff never makes it to the shelves, and those discarded treasures, the items no one saw value in are what I seek out.

Because I'm one too.

Or, at least, that's what Brooks used to say.

My throat tightens, but I ignore it, ignore the fact that I'm one of those discarded items.

Just not a treasure.

Trash that's carefully tossed aside...or into the dumpster.

My hair is tucked up into my hat, my gloves are fully covering my hands, secured by the long sleeves of my black sweater. My leggings are dark and go straight down to my ankles, an inch of which are exposed. I scowl, even knowing I can't do anything about that—I'm tiny, but I *am* wearing another one of those thrift store finds, these being children's leggings. Still, I do my best to tug them down, to cover the slight gap of skin showing.

I know the security system.

But...I need every advantage I can get.

So blending into the shadows.

Wearing all black.

And gloves.

And tucking my hair carefully into my hat.

And—

"Stalling," I whisper softly. And I am.

Because the self-preservation portion of my brain can't imagine I'm doing this. Then again, the self-preservation portion of my brain has shriveled up into nothing over the last years.

Lockpicks in my pocket.

It's just after two in the morning, so the guards will be rotating soon.

Cloudy night. New moon. Guard change.

This will be my only chance.

I squint at the screen of my analog watch—another thrift store find—then up at the house. The shadows shift slightly, and, yup, there they go, the guards pushing away from the wall, walking in pairs.

I move before they disappear around the corner, knowing I have to risk it or I'll be unable to clear the wide expanse of lawn before the next pair of guards comes forward.

As it is, I barely make it into the garden before the new guards round the side of the house.

Heart pounding, I slide between two hedges and try to slow my breathing.

My hands shake, but I clench them into fists, tightly enough to cut off circulation. Tightly enough to bruise. Tightly like I used to hold—

Move.

I pop out of the hedges, cursing internally when the leaves rustle.

It's not a breezy night. There isn't a lot of sound to disguise my movements.

I don't stop, though. Just continue moving until I reach the shadows of the fountain and gazebo. Only then do I breathe. The cameras are focused on the entrance and exit of the maze I am currently making my way through. I can take a second, catch my breath, allow my eyes to adjust to the growing darkness.

There.

Another gap in the hedges, just wide enough for me to squeeze through.

I suck in another silent breath.

Release it.

Move.

This one is tighter, and I have to inch my way through, holding my breath at every rustle, every branch, every crackle of a leaf.

But then I'm through.

And my quarry is just ahead, the French doors of the office dark, hiding the interior of a space I know is filled with leather that is a deep brown and butter soft. Hiding a huge glass and mahogany desk, the gleaming surface always somehow completely free of fingerprints.

Even though he isn't one of those men who pretends to work.

He *works.*

Hard.

That's never in doubt.

Only, the man has to sleep sometime.

Hence why it's two o'clock in the morning and I'm making my approach.

He'll be in bed and—

I glance at my watch, realize I've nearly missed the next interval and burst forward out of the shadows of the hedges, sprinting for the huge potted palms that adorn either side of the entrance.

Not approaching the door—that will be watched on the cameras.

But instead, I move toward the trio of windows on one shadowed wall.

Ivy crawls up the old wooden cases, the glass clear enough that I can see inside, see the shadows of furniture, of the desk.

I left prints on his big, glass-topped desk—from my fingers, my palms, my...ass.

Prints that were cleaned off within the hour.

As though I hadn't existed. As if what I experienced hadn't happened.

A familiar feeling.

Pushing that aside, I tug my picks from my pocket, studying the metal latches. There are sensors on the windows, but I know that the one on the right swells during the summer, the humidity wreaking havoc with the old wood.

The sensor is there, but the contact plate was removed.

That is my way in.

I eye the lock near the latch then select the correct pick from my set, pull out my tension wrench.

Ten seconds later, the pins in the lock have been shifted, the latch opened, and I'm sliding open the heavy sash. I haul myself in, stash away my tools, and close the window almost all the way.

My muscles are screaming from having to drag myself through the opening and my heart pounds, bile rising in my throat. Not from the exertion.

But from being here...in this room, in this place.

It's just another scene in the nightmare that became my life.

But I don't have time for this—for a mental breakdown, for a trip down memory lane. I need to get what I came for, and then I need to get the hell out, and not look back.

Never look back.

Blowing out a silent breath, I take stock of the office.

It's exactly the same, with the exception of books on the shelves lining the far wall.

My breath catches, pulse speeding further.

He doesn't read—hadn't from the moment he got his degree. He had to force himself through too many dry tomes during his college years to ever find joy in it again...or at least, that's what he always told me.

So those shelves filled with books is such a dramatic change that I wonder what the titles are, that I actually take a step in that direction, intending to find out, until I remember myself.

Focus.

Deliberately turning away, I shift behind the desk, ignoring the hint of his cologne—*that* hasn't changed. The scent settles heavy on my senses as I feel for the hidden latch.

It's been a long time and I only saw him do it a handful of times, so it isn't easy—

Click.

The painting behind the desk slides to the side, exposing a steel safe, the black handle basically just shadows in the darkness of the office. But next to it is a silver keypad, the gleam of LEDs nearly blinding.

Throat working, I rise on tiptoe, recall the series of numbers he didn't bother to hide from me, and begin punching them in.

It's been years.

It's likely this won't work, that all of this prep and waiting and sneaking will be for naught.

That the code has been changed and—

Two-six-nine-five. Enter.

The lights on the keypad turn green and there's a soft *click.*

"Holy shit," I whisper and reach for the handle...

Right as an arm winds tightly around my middle and yanks me back against a hard, strong chest.

And I hear Brooks growl,

"What the fuck do you think you're doing?"

THANK YOU FOR READING! I hope you loved Jace and Marie's love story as much as I enjoyed writing it! The next book in the Oak Ridge series is THE BACHELOR & THE BREAK-IN **She's completely wrong for me...but I can't stay away.**

CLICK HERE TO READ THE BACHELOR & THE BREAK-IN NOW>

AND IN THE MEANTIME, do you want more than a taste of those yummy Eagles hockey players? **Once lucky, twice shy. Three times...and I might claim a sexy hockey player as my own. Read** LUCKY LACES now.

AND DO you want a sneak peek into my BRAND NEW hockey series?

If you love big, bearded hockey players who fall hard and fast for the women they love, pick up book one in the Grizzlies Hockey series, MARRIED TO NUMBER TWENTY-TWO NOW>. **I signed the contract. I just didn't expect her to show up ten years later, ready to cash it in.**

CLICK HERE TO READ MARRIED TO NUMBER TWENTY-TWO NOW>

READ on for a sneak peek below!

Aiden

I wake up to a heavy knock on my condo's front door and glare blearily at my phone in the charger.

"Two in the fucking morning," I mutter, grabbing a pillow and clamping it over my ears. "It's two o'clock in the morning on my fucking birthday, and I have to deal with this shit."

This shit being my neighbors.

It's not the first time they've pounded drunk on my door, desperate for their roommate to let them in to what they think is their apartment.

This was sort of funny the first time.

I remember those days, drinking too much, being dumb.

But after the second and the third—where I gained status into the inner circle and a code to the keypad to their apartment door—it was no longer cute.

Now, six months later and countless times of bailing them out, I'm *so* not in the mood.

Especially when it's my fucking birthday.

The knocking cuts off and I think—*pray*—that they've gotten the hint.

But it's approximately two seconds later when it starts up again.

I glance at my phone again, see that really five minutes have passed, making it two-seventeen and officially my birthday.

Some present.

I could try to ignore it—but that just means extending the torture. Sighing, I toss back the blankets and stomp to my apartment door, whipping it open to reveal a slender brunette on my doorstep.

"Ho, mama," she says, gaze taking a slow perusal down my body.

"Who the fuck are you?"

"It's me. Luna."

I stare at her, uncomprehendingly.

"From Rockfield?" she adds.

Recognition begins to dawn. "Luna Maybelle?"

"Yup! That's me." She nods, grinning, and I see it then, the glimpse of my best friend from the childhood rink I grew up playing at come out in her smile. Mischief and life. Joy and hard work.

Summers spent spending every spare moment together—her figure skating, me playing hockey.

But she's not little Luna anymore.

Christ, she's anything but—tall, beautiful, curves for days—and she's staring at me.

Because I'm staring at her.

Fucking hell.

I spur myself into motion.

"Luna! Oh my God!" I pull her into a hug. "What the hell are you doing here?"

"It's your birthday!" She holds up a piece of paper that looks faintly familiar. "And, well, it's mine too, remember?"

That's right.

We have the same birthday.

"We're both twenty-five, single, and—"

My eyes narrow in on the paper. It's crumpled and stained, as though it's years old.

A purple and pink swirl decorates the edges and suddenly I remember her painstakingly drawing it as we sat side-by-side at one of the high top tables of the ice rink, waiting for the Zamboni to finish cutting the ice.

Her brow had been furrowed. Her movements carefully controlled.

And I had been obsessing over how pink her lips were and

what her butt looked like in her skating dress, so much so that I barely remember what we'd been drawing.

No, I think hard, grabbing on to those memories, not what we'd been *drawing*.

The contract we'd put together.

The contract my hormonal twelve-year-old self had signed.

With a sparkly pink colored pencil.

A giant boulder settles in my stomach, but before I can snap myself out of the horror of those memories, she shoves the paper in my hands then throws her arms around my neck.

"We're getting married!"

CLICK HERE TO READ MARRIED TO NUMBER TWENTY-TWO NOW>

OAK RIDGE

Bottles & Blades
Beauty & the Boardroom
The Bachelor & the Break-in

Hate missing Elise's new releases? Love contests, exclusive excerpts and giveaways?
Then signup for Elise's newsletter here!

www.elisefaber.com/newsletter

And join Elise's fan group, the Fabinators (https://www.facebook.com/groups/fabinators) for insider information, sneak peaks at new releases, and fun freebies! Hope to see you there!

If you enjoy my series, considering supporting me on PATREON! Get access to early releases, bonus content, character art, audiobooks, special edition covers, swag, and much more!

CLICK HERE TO SUPPORT ME>

I so appreciate your help in spreading the word about my books, including sharing with friends! Please leave a review on your favorite book site!

ALSO BY ELISE FABER

***Gold Hockey* (all stand alone)**

Blocked

Backhand

Boarding

Benched

Breakaway

Breakout

Checked

Coasting

Centered

Charging

Caged

Crashed

A Gold Christmas

Cycled

Caught

Cap

Covered

Crushed

Changed

Scored

Breakers Hockey (all stand alone)

Broken

Boldly

Breathless

Ballsy

Bewitched

Blowout

Breathe

Blazed

Sierra Hockey Series

Over the Line

Caught from Behind

The Big Skate

On the Fly

Eagles Hockey Series (all stand alone)

Broken Laces

Lace 'em Up

Knotted Laces

Loaded Laces

Lucky Laces

Oak Ridge Vineyards

Bottles & Blades

Beauty & the Boardroom

The Bachelor & the Break-in

Rush Hockey Trilogy #1

Big Puck Energy

Filthy Puckboy

So Pucking Over It

Rush Hockey Trilogy #2

Love, Pucks, and Other Stories

All's Fair in Pucks and War

No Pucks Lost Between Us

Rush Hockey Novellas

Puck and Make Up

Billionaire's Club (all stand alone)

Bad Night Stand

Bad Breakup

Bad Husband

Bad Hookup

Bad Divorce

Bad Fiancé

Bad Boyfriend

Bad Blind Date

Bad Wedding

Bad Engagement

Bad Bridesmaid

Bad Swipe

Bad Girlfriend

Bad Best Friend

Bad Rebound

Bad Romance

Bad Business

Bad Billionaire's Quickies

Love, Action, Camera (all stand alone)

Dotted Line

Action Shot

Close-Up

End Scene

Meet Cute

Love After Midnight **(all stand alone)**

Rum And Notes

Virgin Daiquiri

On The Rocks

Sex On The Seats

Life Sucks Series

Train Wreck

Hot Mess

Dumpster Fire

Clusterf*@k

FUBAR

Perfect Storm

Free Fall

Lost Cause

Roosevelt Ranch Series **(all stand alone, series complete)**

Disaster at Roosevelt Ranch

Heartbreak at Roosevelt Ranch

Collision at Roosevelt Ranch

Regret at Roosevelt Ranch

Desire at Roosevelt Ranch

***Phoenix Series* (read in order)**

Phoenix Rising

Dark Phoenix

Phoenix Freed

***Phoenix: LexTal Chronicles* (rereleasing soon, stand alone, Phoenix world)**

From Ashes

In Flames

To Smoke

KTS Series (all stand alone, series complete)

Riding The Edge

Crossing The Line

Leveling The Field

Scorching The Earth

Cocky Heroes World

Tattooed Troublemaker

ABOUT THE AUTHOR

USA Today bestselling author, Elise Faber, loves chocolate, Star Wars, Harry Potter, and hockey (the order depending on the day and how well her team -- the Sharks! -- are playing). She and her husband also play as much hockey as they can squeeze into their schedules, so much so that their typical date night is spent on the ice. Elise is the mom to two exuberant boys and lives in Northern California. Connect with her in her Facebook group, the Fabinators or find more information about her books at www.elisefaber.com.

facebook.com/elisefaberauthor

amazon.com/author/elisefaber

bookbub.com/profile/elise-faber

instagram.com/elisefaber

tiktok.com/@elisefaberauthor

goodreads.com/elisefaber